QUESTIONS, QUARRELS, & QUANDARY

A Camper And Criminals Cozy Mystery

Book Thirty Two

BY
TONYA KAPPES

TONYA KAPPES
WEEKLY NEWSLETTER

Want a behind-the-scenes journey of me as a writer?
The ups and downs, new deals, book sales, giveaways and more? I share it all! Join the exclusive Southern Sleuths private group today! Go to www.patreon.com/Tonyakappesbooks

As a special thank you for joining, you'll get an exclusive copy of my cross-over short story, *A CHARMING BLEND.* Go to Tonyakappes.com and click on subscribe at the top of the home page.

Laughter and lighthearted chatter filled the undercroft, our little group becoming the life of the party. With friends like these, who wouldn't feel blessed?

As everyone at the tables continued to devour the delicious Southern delicacies, I heard an unmistakable sound, a crackling voice that made my heart lurch. It was the squawk of Hank's police scanner, a device he stubbornly refused to part ways with even after leaving the force—a reminder of his past and a tether to the world he once served.

The familiar hum of the scanner seemed alien amidst the cheerful banter and clinking cutlery. Betts, Abby, Dottie, Queenie, and I all instinctively swiveled in our seats toward the source. We listened to the police scanner every day down at the laundromat.

Hank, his brows furrowed, pulled the compact device from his pocket and held it up to his ear.

"What's the buzz, Hank?" I asked, my heart pounding.

His confusion was palpable, his gaze distant.

"Is it your missing teen case?" I tried to keep my voice steady, even though my mind was racing with all sorts of horrible scenarios.

The silence that followed felt as heavy as a church bell. "No... It's

Etta Hardgrove. She's... She's dead." His voice was somber, the words lingering in the air like an ominous fog.

Dottie was the first to break the silence. "Well, ain't that a kick in the pants!" She sprang to her feet, her hand snatching her cigarette case and the remaining slice of pie from the table. "No rest for the wicked, ladies!"

CHAPTER ONE

The first rays of dawn were just giving the sky a good morning kiss when I pushed myself out of the cozy confines of my camper van. The world was still quiet, the birds just clearing their throats for the morning chorus. Now, a lady doesn't often get up with the chickens, but that day had a special kind of promise to it. The kind that whistled through the pines and waltzed with the honeysuckle perfume in the air at Happy Trails Campground.

You see, my friend Dottie Swagger, the manager of Happy Trails, had a fancy for yard sales that would put a starved coonhound on a ham hock to shame. And in this part of Normal, Kentucky, located deep in the Daniel Boone National Forest, where kudzu draped over everything that held still long enough, we cherished yard sales like a preacher did his Bible.

In this town, every old bit and bob wasn't just an artifact; it was a cipher of tales whispered in hushed reverence. As Dottie liked to say, "These ain't just knickknacks, sugar. They're whole lives, stories in brass and porcelain just waiting to be dusted off."

The two of us had seen more sunrises over a cup of Trails Coffee special blend than a rooster on an insomniac's farm, always eager for the Saturday edition of the *Normal Gazette*'s special yard sale section.

After all, the early bird got the choicest pickings, and Dottie wasn't one to lose out on a juicy find.

Dottie had a knack for it, I'll tell you. The way she would stroll through those laid-out wares, you would think she was at a debutante ball instead of trawling through dusty, forgotten treasures. And it wasn't just the thrill of a bargain that got her heart ticking. It was the stories, the hidden narratives behind every tarnished silver locket and faded family photograph, that set her eyes alight.

We found ourselves sipping our warm brews, our attention focused on one advertisement in particular.

"Benson Estate Sale. Starts at dawn. Early birds get the worms." Dottie hummed.

Beneath the awning of my vintage camper van, Dottie and I sat at my picnic table.

"Look at us." Dottie snickered. "We're perched like two hens on a fence." She fanned her cigaretted hand in front of her face. "It's gonna be a hot one. It's only six a.m., and the air is already as thick as molasses."

"Lots of picnic-sitting this week." I clicked my tongue and looked out onto the lake located smack-dab in the center of Happy Trails Campground. I lifted my mug to my lips and took in all the empty camper lots that would soon be filled by a group of traveling women, Camper Cowgirls.

From what I'd learned about them, they were a nationwide camping organization for women only whose ages spanned several decades and who came together as a group that loved to camp.

"Come on, Fifi!" I called to my toy poodle, who had gone on her own sniff walk.

My picnic table was strewn with the detritus of our summer Saturday-morning routine: coffee mugs still steaming with the dregs of brew and the *Normal Gazette* laid out before us like a map to treasure.

Dottie, the spectacle of our morning ritual, sat in her faded house-coat, her head a constellation of pink sponge curlers. Between her fingers, a cigarette smoldered, the smoke spiraling upward around the loose tendrils of hair escaping from her curlers.

She took a thoughtful drag on her cigarette, the tip blazing bright against the morning's soft glow. The exhaled smoke curled up and away, mingling with the humid Kentucky air. With her other hand, she gently unrolled one curler, setting loose a ringlet.

"Woo-wee," she cackled. "My hair is as bouncy and lively as a square dance today."

Her gaze, sharp as a barber's razor, was fixed on the newspaper, scanning the yard sale section with a focus that would put a cat on a mouse hole to shame. I swear, she could spot a promising sale from a mile away, just by the look of the ad in the *Gazette*.

"Lookie here!" she squealed in delight. "Curb alert at Etta Hard-grove's!"

"Curb alert?" I asked, watching Dottie in awe. It was an art, really, the way she balanced that cigarette, the curler removal, and her fierce concentration on the newspaper.

"Oh yeah. Curb alerts are gold for free things, and Etta has the best items for free." The cherry of her cigarette glowed in concert with the fiery trail of her freshly released curls, the newspaper rustling like dried leaves as she folded it in half and stuck it up underneath her armpit.

"I guess we are going," I said. I knew Dottie was serious about the curb alert when she snuffed out her half-smoked cigarette. It's the only time she would leave a smoke without giving it a proper send-off.

"Well, I reckon you didn't hear me. I said"—and she pronounced her next words using her lips in dramatic fashion—"*currrb a-lerrt*. The mere mention of it sets my heart fluttering like a hummingbird in a flower patch. I told you Etta has got some real good stuff, and we've got to go before anyone else beats us to the punch."

"What about the Bensons?" I asked. They were the oldest, wealthiest folks in town. They'd made so many donations to the Daniel Boone National Forest that my office in the national park building, where I was on the park committee, was named after the Bensons. "Their collection is sure to have some intriguing pieces, and it's closer than where Etta Hargrove lives."

"I don't care. You said you'd go with me today, and today is the day. I've been waiting for Etta to have another one." She clicked her tongue and clapped her hands to get Fifi's attention. "Let's get a treat!" she hollered, getting Fifi to run at full speed back to the camper.

"We have to be back by noon. The Camping Cowgirls are supposed to be here to check in for the week, and Betts will be here with the church van to take everyone to a late lunch at the Normal Diner." I reminded Dottie of the large group reservation she'd made—and all the plans she'd agreed to without asking me, even though I was the one who would be making sure they were all accommodated.

"Time to shake a leg and skedaddle," Dottie said, even putting Fifi in the camper van and returning with my keys. "That curb alert ain't gonna plunder itself!"

The anticipation was as thick as good gravy on biscuits. Dottie jumped into my little car, housecoat and all, and we set off, armed with pocketbooks and sturdy shopping bags.

Dottie was a lady on a mission, little guessing that amongst those dusty relics, we were about to unearth a mystery that would turn our cozy campground life on its ear. But hey, that was life in Normal, where nothing was normal.

CHAPTER TWO

Dottie couldn't stop smiling.

Every once in a while, she'd take a look in the rearview mirror as she rode shotgun in my Ford, her eyes swooping up to the car roof. Dottie had found an old lawn chair she just couldn't resist from Etta's curb alert. Like an old trophy, it was strapped to the top of my little four-door, the chair's fabric fading and worn but full of character —just like Dottie herself. She was so proud of it that she couldn't stop talking about how good it was going to look outside her camper.

"Well, butter my biscuits and call me a roll, will ya?" Dottie exclaimed as we turned into the entrance of Happy Trails and drove up the gravel road leading to the campground.

I couldn't help but smile. If there was one thing that tickled Dottie more than a good deal, it was the sight of vintage campers.

It has been a few years now, but when I first moved to Happy Trails Campground as the owner, I knew it would make a wonderful resort and retreat not just for people who owned a camper but also for folks who wanted the experience of a camper without owning one. That's how I came up with the idea of redoing a lot of little vintage campers and renting them out. So they held a soft spot in Dottie's heart and mine.

Lining both sides of the gravel road, at least ten vintage campers stood proudly, each one as unique as its owner. And they were ten minutes early. The Camping Cowgirl group, known for its vintage-camper parade, was nothing if not punctual.

"Ain't they a sight for sore eyes?" Dottie said, her eyes twinkling as she gazed at the procession.

Some campers were polished to a shine and painted in vibrant hues, like the turquoise one with pink flamingos on the side that was my personal favorite. Others bore their age proudly, their original paint jobs chipped and faded but no less beautiful.

"They're a work of art, every single one of them," I agreed, my gaze lingering on a camper done up in a retro Coca-Cola theme, complete with a red-and-white color scheme and vintage bottle decals.

"Land sakes alive, Mae!" Dottie suddenly exclaimed, pointing a painted fingernail at a small green camper with original wooden panels. "Look at that li'l pea pod! Ain't she a hoot?"

The sight of these nostalgic tin cans on wheels, each with its own unique story to tell, made a familiar warmth spread through my chest. This was my home. The place I'd chosen. Eccentric neighbors, charming campers, and all the Southern charm a girl could ask for.

The sun was shining, and my campground was coming to life with the colorful hustle and bustle of the Camping Cowgirl group. As I unbuckled my seat belt, I couldn't help but think that this was going to be one heck of a day.

I was greeted by a woman hanging out of her truck as soon as I parked the car and got out. "We are early," she said. "We would've pulled up to our campsites, but we didn't know which one was which."

"No problem. Let me get the paperwork." I smiled and glanced back at my car, where Dottie was busying herself with the straps to retrieve her prized possession, the lawn chair, from the roof of the car. "Dottie! Leave it!" I called and waved her over to come help me.

Part of Dottie's job as the manager and mine as the owner was to check guests in and out. Most of our check-ins were on Sunday, but this week was special, and everything started today.

It was the annual 127 Yard Sale, the longest yard sale in the States, running from Michigan to Alabama through six states and cutting right through Normal.

The actual event was only four days, but that was for the registered vendors and main shops and didn't include all the folks in houses dotting the roads through the small towns who set their own items out to make a buck or two. Why not? It was a no-brainer to use the big bucks spent in advertising for the six hundred ninety-mile event when you lived along the route. Many times during the year, I'd hear from locals how they were waiting for the annual sale to put out things they no longer needed.

"Looks like you already started picking." One of the Camping Cowgirls pointed to my car when Dottie walked over.

"Oh yeah." Dottie tucked her thumbs in the pocket of her housecoat and rocked back on the worn heels of her flip-flops. "That there was free as in f-r-e-e." She spelled out the word as though it was worth gold.

"We haven't come across anything for free," another Camping Cowgirl chimed in as she hung out the window of her SUV, a little Bubble Airstream hooked behind.

"Have y'all been traveling a long way?" I asked the one who seemed like the head of the group as she came inside the office with me.

"We came from Ohio. Not too far. We like to head through Kentucky and try to make it through Tennessee, but these mountains get us every time." She snorted. "Charlotte Taylor," she introduced herself. "I'm the informal leader of this group."

"How fun." I had so many questions, but I'd let them get settled and use the lure of the campfire tonight to find out all their personal information.

Over the years, I'd learned more about my fellow campers around fires than anywhere else. Stories were shared, laughter became contagious, and more often than not, life's wisdom was exchanged alongside the flicker of flames and the comfort of shared silence. Under the star-speckled blanket of the night sky, with the gentle crackle of a campfire as a soundtrack, guarded expressions will soften and people can truly open up.

I retrieved the folder with their paperwork and opened it to go over with her. "If you want to look over your reservation and make sure the next of kin is filled out." Even though she had put all ten camping reservations on one credit card, I still had to have the information.

I gestured for Charlotte to sit at one of the chairs in front of my desk. I walked around the desk and sat in my chair. "Please let me know if anyone has pets. We have these to put in your camper window in case of an emergency."

I pulled out a couple of the animal signs I had my guests put in their windows for if they weren't in their camper when there was a fire or if something happened to the guests themselves, so emergency workers would know there was a pet inside.

"Bea has a cat." She took one of the cat signs. "I'll be sure to give it to her. She's the one with the trailer inspired by Coca-Cola."

"I noticed it right off." My eyes glowed as I wondered what I needed to do to get a tour of the inside.

"Bea is the free spirit of the group. She was an artist by profession, a talent that is clearly reflected in her camper." Charlotte laughed while talking of her friend. "That mop of curly hair is always a different color, every trip we take. She decided to go with lavender this time."

"She and Dottie will get along just fine." I nodded out the window where Dottie was already making fast friends with Bea.

Bea and Dottie were laughing. Bea had a radiant smile, and you could tell she had a zest for life by her array of vibrant, mismatched clothes and chunky jewelry. Bea was as colorful and captivating as the art she created with her travel trailer.

"Is that a 1960 Shasta Compact?" I asked about Bea's trailer.

"Oh yeah. She loves that darn thing. And Coke." Charlotte got up and handed me the closed file. "Everything looks to be in order."

"Great. Let me get you a copy." I took it and moved to the printer.

"Don't worry about it right now. I'll be here a few days, so you can just give it to me later." She turned toward the door. "I think the gals are a bit antsy to set up and get ready for our lunch at the Normal Diner. They are excited to go to a few antiques shops around here."

"Sounds good." I followed her to the door and reached around to open it for her. "I'll see y'all back here. My friend Betts is going to bring her church van so we can all go together."

"That sounds perfect." Charlotte led the way out of the office.

"Nice to meet you, Charlotte." I handed her a brochure that included the guest rules and a map of the campground.

"Charlie," she corrected me. "My mom calls me Charlotte, and she's been long dead." She waved her arms at the chuckwagon of the Camping Cowgirls to follow her as the lead car through the campground, where they all found their camping spots one after the other.

"This is going to be a lively bunch." Dottie rubbed her hands together. "We are going to have some fun, ain't we?"

"I think we sure are," I said and waved at each trailer driving past the office.

Dottie and I watched the orchestrated chaos from our vantage point at the recreational outdoor area, sipping some sweet iced tea she'd retrieved from her camper.

The Camping Cowgirls unhitched their vintage trailers with practiced ease. They connected to the full hookup the campground offered, making sure water, electric, and sewage lines were securely attached. All around us, the tranquil beauty of the national park—soaring trees, blooming wildflowers, and the gentle chirping of birds—added a serene backdrop to the unfolding scene.

"You gotta hand it to these gals, Mae. They know their way 'round a trailer hitch better than most men I've seen," Dottie observed, a note of approval in her voice.

"I reckon you're right, Dottie," I agreed, admiring their efficiency and camaraderie.

Our attention then drifted to Henry Bryant, the maintenance employee of Happy Trails, and Beck Greer, the enthusiastic young teenager who spent his summers working at the campground. Under the unforgiving sun, their faces were flushed with excitement as they put finishing touches on their surprise for the Camping Cowgirls.

They'd transformed our usual laid-back tiki hut into a celebration of cowgirl spirit. There were brightly colored bandanas tied to the rafters, fluttering gently in the breeze. Strings of fairy lights, each covered with tiny cowboy-boot-and-hat motifs, were strung up around the hut and along the pathways, promising a beautiful spectacle once the sun set. Picnic tables were covered in red-and-white-checkered tablecloths, lending a rustic charm to the setup.

In one corner of the area, a large, wooden sign hand-painted by Beck proudly declared Welcome, Camping Cowgirls! and was adorned with a detailed drawing of a cowgirl astride a horse against a background of towering mountains and wide-open plains.

Hay bales, each topped with a plush blanket and plump cushion, were strategically placed around the fire pits, providing additional seating and adding to the overall theme.

"Would you look at that, Dottie? Those boys have really outdone themselves," I said, marveling at their creativity and effort.

"Well, as sure as eggs is eggs, they've done a fine job, haven't they?" Dottie agreed, her voice filled with admiration.

Underneath the clear blue sky, amid the splendor of the national park, it was a perfect day at the Happy Trails Campground. As the Camping Cowgirls got settled, the air filled with anticipation and laughter.

Gravel spitting up underneath some tires joined the sounds of the ladies chattering. I turned around to see who was coming and smiled when I saw the Normal Baptist Church van with Betts Hager in the driver's seat.

Betts threw her hand up in a big wave before she pulled in next to my car to park. When she got out of the van, I couldn't help but smile when I noticed her glow.

It'd been a long time since I'd seen her look that way. Betts was one of those people who was all things to everyone but herself. Not only had she been married to a preacher, which came with its own set of challenges, but then he had committed an unthinkable crime that'd sent him to jail, leaving her heartbroken and feeling that her marriage was a sham. She took her role as a preacher's wife very seriously, and she had ingrained her entire self into the community to make it perfect for the church's congregation as well.

As if that wasn't enough, she also had to endure her ex-husband succumbing to an illness, leaving her with the tasks of having to forgive him and take on his final do-gooder list to complete deeds he'd left behind.

Through it all, Betts did find a new relationship with a local man, Ryan Rivera, and I couldn't help but wonder if the huge smile on her face wasn't due to him.

"You look adorable." I had to compliment her since the last few months she'd been wearing baggy clothes, not fixing her hair or even taking care of herself at all.

That day, her green off-the-shoulder peasant top was tucked in the front of a pair of white shorts. She'd even styled her brown, chin-length hair into loose waves. Blunt bangs hung above her sparkling brown eyes.

"Well, bless my buttered biscuits." Dottie's Southern twang spilled out as soon as she noticed what I noticed.

Only I didn't make a big deal out of it like Dottie did.

"You're lookin' so good, you could charm the pants off a picky old coonhound! Did that makeover of yours have somethin' to do with that handsome fella Ryan?" Dottie continued to look Betts up and down.

"Maybe." Betts sighed and pretended to flutter her eyes. "We actually finished all of Lester's do-gooder list, and ever since then, I've been able to sleep all night. Which has made me get clearer-headed."

"Does this mean you and Ryan are an officially official couple?" I asked, patting my hands over my unruly curls. The humidity in the air was starting to dampen my hair, which left it a springy mess.

"Yes." Betts bounced up and down on her toes. "It's so silly. I feel like a teenager in love again."

"Don't you dare say silly," I told her and gave her a hug. "That's the best feeling in the world. I remember when I first started to date Hank, I felt the same way, and then I asked myself, why on earth would I diminish how I feel about him and how happy he makes me?"

"I knew it the moment you laid eyes on that boy," Dottie said, referring to Hank. She'd been there since day one. As in, the day I drove the camper van into Happy Trails and parked right next to the small dock.

The memory played in my head like it was yesterday. Much like today, the sun was shining, the humidity had my hair all up in a curly mess, and I'd not showered for two days. I was standing on the dock overlooking the murky lake with a layer of moss all over the surface, wondering how on earth I was going to make the place sellable so I could go back to my pampered life in New York City, when Hank's big black car came barreling up the campground road. He jumped out, and from that first moment we met, his piercing green eyes made my heart go pitter-patter. Even when he accused me of harboring my ex who'd broken out of prison and threatened to arrest me, there was something deep down in me that was still attracted to him.

That was the look I remembered, and it sure did feel like the look on Betts's face right then. She was snookered.

"Lord, he must be sweeter than a jar of homemade apple pie to make you shine like a freshly polished pickup truck." Dottie made Betts laugh more and bat her lashes even faster. "Keep flutterin' them eyelashes, honey, and you'll have him wrapped around your little finger tighter than a snake in a knot!"

"Oh, Dottie. I could carry on with you for days." Betts literally couldn't stop smiling. "He does make me happy." Her eyes drifted past me and Dottie. "Speaking of happy, those little campers are adorable."

"Those are the Camping Cowgirls, the group you're taking to town." I glanced over to the very dock that'd given way the day I first laid eyes on Hank. Some of the Camping Cowgirls were standing there and chatting away.

"Mae, you go get them, and I'm going to show Betts my new chair." Dottie curled her hand into Betts's elbow, dragging her away to my car.

She wasn't fooling me any. Dottie was using Betts to help her carry it over to Dottie's camper.

As I walked down the campground toward my camper van to get Fifi, pride washed over me. The midday sun had turned the Daniel Boone National Forest into a picture straight out of a beautiful, nostalgic painting, giving it the best possible backdrop for Happy Trails, one I was hoping these ladies would remember.

I glanced across the shimmering body of water. The Camping Cowgirls's vintage campers looked like little nuggets of the past, splashed with color and brimming with stories. A warmth spread through me from knowing I was providing a home for those campers as their adventurous owners explored the longest yard sale along the 127.

I reached my camper van, a familiar presence nestled amongst the towering trees. "All right, girl," I said to Fifi, who was already standing at the screen door. "You want to go bye-bye?"

Her little tail wiggled so fast that her legs danced with anticipation. She loved going for rides.

"Let's show these ladies what Normal has to offer," I said and took a step into the camper van to make sure Fifi was looking her finest. "What about the mini camper's shirt?"

I plucked one of Fifi's many little outfits from the basket right inside the door near the passenger's captain seat, which I kept turned around for guests. With one good whip of the wrist, the shirt snapped into form.

Fifi's nails ticked along the vinyl flooring as the excitement cursed through her tiny, furry body. I sat on the floor to let her scurry up to me. She loved looking so fancy. She was born and bred to be a prestigious show dog, but Ethel Biddle's old dog and Fifi had had other plans. They did have the cutest set of puppies, but I learned my lesson.

If Fifi was going to be a campground dog and run around, she had to be fixed. And that marked the end of her pedigreed-dog career.

With Fifi in tow and her leash in my hand, I headed back to the meeting point, taking one last look at the serene lake reflecting the myriad colors of the vintage campers. It was peaceful.

Betts and Dottie had started to round up the Camping Cowgirls to board the church bus so we could get on with our tour of downtown Normal.

Dottie Swagger, her cigarette smoke spiraling up in the warm air, was adding humor to the group, chatting them up one by one as they got on the bus. I had no idea what she was saying, but I was sure it was hilarious by the way they were laughing in response.

Dottie clicked her tongue when she saw Fifi. Fifi took off toward her. Even the fur babies loved Dottie.

I headed to the storage units just beyond Dottie's camper and right across from the office where the bus was parked to talk to Henry. I found him in the one unit we used for all the seasonal things we had to store. The other units were rented by seasonal campers.

We only allowed ten camping sites to be leased by seasonal campers. Some of them stayed yearly while others just rented them for a season, left their campers, and came on various weekends during their rental to get away from life for a while.

The only yearly tenants we had were Henry, Dottie, me, Hank and Ty Randal. But Ty and Ellis, Hank's sister—along with Ty's dad and young siblings—were about to embark on a new journey: owning a house.

I snickered at the thought and considered how far I'd come from when I thought living in a camper was the most ridiculous thing I'd ever heard of.

"Henry, we're about to leave," I said when I walked into the storage unit where he and Beck appeared to be rearranging boxes. "I don't think anyone else is checking in until tomorrow, but do you mind keeping an eye on the place?"

"Now, you know I don't mind," Henry grumbled, a soft note of resignation in his voice. "Beck here can finish off stacking the boxes."

I glanced around and pointed to the stack in the front that had Wedding written on them in black marker. My mind curled back to all the things I'd been collecting over the past year for my upcoming wedding to Hank.

Mary Elizabeth, my foster-adoptive mama, had insisted I have a proper Southern wedding in a real wedding venue, not a campground. So she seemed to have been satisfied when I'd agreed to have the reception at the Old Train Station Motel, where there was a barn repurposed for such things.

"Don't be messing with those," I teased when I left the two alone to head back to the church bus.

We were about to embark on what I hoped would be a memorable day, filled with antiques shops and fun stories. As I stepped up on the bus and rounded the corner to join the others, a sudden chill raced down my spine. It seemed out of place, jarring in the otherwise calm day.

Dottie patted the seat next to her. "What's with that look?" Dottie asked over the sound of Betts closing the bus door and the chatter of the ladies sitting behind us.

I looked past Dottie out the window at the forest, the lake, and the sun-soaked campers across the campground. Nothing looked out of sorts, but the stillness was almost ominous.

"Nothing," I responded and shook my head, a sense of unease creeping over me, an unsettling inkling that something was about to go wrong, just when everything was going so right.

CHAPTER THREE

As we drove through the verdant canopy of the Daniel Boone National Forest toward downtown Normal, Dottie Swagger was putting on a real show for the Camping Cowgirls. I mean, she was laying it on so thick that *I* was excited, even though I'd been there a million times.

"Now, ladies," she said, her Southern accent wrapping around each word like a warm, familiar blanket, "we got some real treasures here in Normal. Y'all ain't gonna believe your eyes!"

She gestured animatedly with a hand laden by an unlit cigarette as she launched into her enthusiastic description. "First up, we got Deters Feed-n-Seed, run by our very own Alvin Deters. Now, don't let the name fool ya. He's got the most unique collection of camping items this side of the Mississippi. Makes you feel like you're stepping into an adventure every time you walk through them doors."

A chorus of oohs and aahs greeted Dottie's words. I watched from my seat, feeling a swell of pride for our little town.

"Now, when we get to the Tough Nickel Thrift Shop, y'all are gonna be like kids in a candy store. The saying goes, 'One man's junk is another man's treasure,' right? Well, darlin's, it ain't never been truer than it is at the Tough Nickel. You can find everything from vintage cowboy boots to old-timey cookware. And who knows what other treasures are waitin' for you?"

Her eyes sparkled with a kind of excitement that was contagious. "And between y'all and me," she added, her voice dropping conspiratorially, "the heart of our town ain't just the shops. See that grassy median separating the one-way streets? It's like our own little oasis right in the middle of downtown. Shady picnic tables, perfect for a summer lunch, and that amphitheater... well, it's seen more laughter and joy than you could shake a stick at."

As the church bus pulled into downtown, a large, colorful sign came into view. It read Welcome Camping Cowgirls, and it made the ladies in the bus cheer. It felt like home, like community. And as that odd chill from before tried to creep back up my spine, I shrugged it off and exited the bus with the others. We were in for a good day, I was certain.

At least, I hoped.

"Look at the smiles on all their faces," Gert Hobson said as she stood in the front window of her store, Trails Coffee Shop. She held a steaming-hot cup of coffee in one hand while the other was situated on her hip.

Fifi had wandered over to the dog bowl Gert left out for all the fur babies. During the summer, she always put out a few bowls of food and water both outside and inside.

"No, no," I called out to Fifi to take her attention away from the living wall on her way back to me.

The living wall was a unique feature Gert Hobson had added with great consideration, enlisting an architect to create the design in her imagination. It was a full wall of the seasonal flowers and foliage that grew up around the Daniel Boone National Forest and Gert's way of thanking Mother Nature for the great shop it afforded her.

Without what the forest had to offer for nature enthusiasts, Gert always swore she'd never have been successful. The truth was, Gert was so successful that she'd even had her coffee pirated by one of the biggest coffee chains in the world, and through somewhat of a hassle, she got the rights back and a nice payout, which didn't have anything to do with where Trails Coffee was located.

Hands down, she did have the best coffee and the best blends I'd ever had.

Then again, I might be biased.

"Dottie sure has taken a shine to them camping women," I said in my best Dottie accent and pointed out to the grassy median where Dottie was leading them like she was a tour guide. "I thought I would stop in here while she took them around the park."

"It was very nice of Preacher Alex to offer the church van," Gert noted, calling our newest and youngest preacher by his first name.

"I think it was more of Betts's idea than his. I'm not so sure he is on my side or would at least talk to God for me if I was in a pinch, not after he got shot." I reminded her of how my curiosity got the Laundry Club Ladies and me stuck in the middle of a murder investigation and how we sorta left a criminal seeking sanctuary in the church with Preacher Alex Elliott, which only led a killer to the church who had no regard for the house of God... and no issue shooting the preacher.

"He's a man of God," Gert said of Alex, turning to look at me. "I'm sure he's forgiven you."

"I wouldn't be so sure." I smiled and excused myself when I noticed Dottie leading the charge away from the amphitheater.

They all stopped at the fun sign Abby Fawn Bonds, my sister-in-law, had made and put up in the Camping Cowgirls's honor. We'd had to get the mayor's approval, which wasn't too hard because Abby explained it was a great marketing idea to entice other camping groups to come to Normal.

It was truly a spectacular summer day, and downtown Normal was a sight to behold. Nestled in the embrace of the Daniel Boone National Forest, it was like stepping into a different world where time moved a little slower and every nook and cranny told a story of its own.

Each local business was housed in a quaint cottage, complete with white picket fences that made the heart swell with warm nostalgia. The homespun charm of the place was as inviting as a sweet summer breeze. And just beyond, the majestic forest loomed, a constant reminder of the beautiful wildness that coexisted with our small-town charm.

Laughter spilled from the side yard of Trails Coffee, which was filled with customers sipping on Gert's delicious offerings as they sat at the café tables, enjoying the warm day.

There wasn't hardly an inch available in the grassy median that cut through the center of downtown, the park-like setting that was a testament to Normal's love for nature. The jewel of that verdant oasis was the amphitheater. Its tall pillars stood proudly amidst the greenery, draped in hanging baskets of ferns that swayed gently in the breeze.

Even the carriage lights had their own character. They dotted the sidewalk, and at night they cast a warm glow over the lively area. Each carriage light was accompanied by a dowel rod, one side bearing a basket bursting with colorful summer flowers and the other side waving a cheerful summer banner. It was as if the town itself was celebrating the season.

Everywhere you looked, people were soaking in the beauty of Normal.

"Excuse me," someone said when they accidentally bumped into me on the bustling sidewalk. I reached down to pick up Fifi, fearing she was going to be trampled. "I'm sorry."

"No. Please. I'm sorry," I said. "I was just standing here in everyone's way." I put my hand up over my eyes, shielding them from the bright sun, and I noticed it was Etta Hardgrove.

Her black hair was swept up into a meticulous bun, streaked with dignified shades of grey that hinted at her life experiences. Her clear sea-green eyes sparkled with a mix of wisdom and mischief, ready to share a story or two if you had the time to listen.

"Etta," I greeted her.

Her face, while touched by the gentle hands of time, was remarkably smooth. Every wrinkle, every laugh line, seemed to add to her charm rather than diminish it. Her high cheekbones and strong jawline gave her an air of authority, while her ever-present smile kept her approachable.

"Oh, Mae. I'm so sorry. I was on a mission with this old stuff." She patted a bag she had thrown over her shoulder. The contents clanked as she swung it around and let it land between her feet on the ground. She put her hands on her hips and leaned back into a stretch before she popped up again. She was of average height, yet her straight posture and the confident way she held herself made her seem taller.

Etta was stout, her body having filled out with age, but it was a robustness that suited her. It gave the impression of a woman who had stood her ground in the face of life's trials and had come out stronger. "Lots of junk in here." She patted the bag. Her bold earrings swung back and forth, grazing the top of the floral-print blouse she had tucked super tightly in a pair of khaki slacks. "Who's this little baby?" She literally took Fifi out of my arms.

Fifi must have taken a liking to Etta, because the dog started to lick all over her face.

"Fifi, stop that." I tried to make her quit, but Etta continued to coax her with kissy lips, so I just threw in the towel.

"Aren't you just the tiniest, cutest thang evah?" Etta's Southern drawl showed a little more as she talked.

I couldn't help but notice her hands as she ran them down Fifi's fur. She wasn't afraid of work, and the small scars on them told a story of a life lived with gusto, the marks probably from baking, gardening, and just plain-old everyday living.

"I'm taking them to Buck because he can probably get a little more for them on consignment than I can get from a group of cheapskates like them, only here for the trillion-mile-long yard sale." She pointed her chin toward the oncoming Camping Cowgirls. "I better hurry if Buck is going to get this stuff out before they get in there."

"Bye, Etta." She hurried off toward the Tough Nickel, and I laughed, not having time to tell her the Camping Cowgirls were at Happy Trails

Campground this week. I wasn't even sure if she heard me tell her goodbye.

"Hello, Mae!" Helen Pyle called across the grassy median from the Cute-icles salon. "I've got you and Mary Elizabeth down for a facial and haircut tomorrow!"

"We'll be there!" I called back with a wave, having totally forgotten I was supposed to spend the full day with Mary Elizabeth tomorrow. By "full," I mean it started at eleven a.m. at church. I'd promised her that I'd go to church and then go with her to Cute-icles, where Helen had a special day planned for the church ladies on Sunday.

"Your town is adorable," Charlie said with a delighted tone as she walked by, following Dottie, and grabbed my arm to drag me with her. Fifi hurried alongside us, her leash pulled taut. "We are so thrilled with Dottie. She's a funny one."

"Yes. She's her own little must-see attraction." I nodded.

"And look at these display windows." One of the women pointed to a particular shop.

"Each shop window is a testament to the creativity and passion of its owners." I sounded like the brochure we had on display for our little town in the campground office.

Charlie and her friend pointed out a shop where there was a vintage hammock adorned with summer reads strung between two wooden pillars. Another had an impressive collection of sun hats, each more colorful than the last.

"Edna, have you met Mae? Properly?" Charlie asked her friend before she started in on the introductions. "I know you know she's in charge of the campground."

"I own it." For some reason, I took so much pride in my little part of Happy Trails. "Dottie, now, she's the one who runs it."

"She's amazing." Edna rolled her eyes as a fervent expression of Dottie love.

As I walked down the vibrant sidewalk with them, I couldn't help but feel a deep sense of love for my town as they went on and on about it. Truthfully, someone could pick up Normal and plop it down in a different place, and it would be just like any other town. It was the feeling there that made it a special place.

And I was so proud to call it home.

"Gosh, these shops and this town are wonderful. A true gem." Edna gasped. "And to think, I thought I had amazing places to visit."

"What do you do?" I was curious.

"In books, honey." Edna peered over the rim of what I thought looked like reading

glasses. "I'm a retired librarian." She was soft-spoken.

"My sister-in-law is the librarian here." The tone of my voice lightened with glee. "She says she never needs to travel because she goes to so many places every day in her books."

"She's right. Books can take you everywhere. But I do love a good camping trip." She winked and tucked some wispy gray hairs back into her low bun.

"I'm happy you're here." I wanted them to know how delightful I found them to be. "Which camper is yours?"

"1955 Airstream Bubble," she said, full of confidence about her rare camper.

I squealed.

"You want to look inside?"

I nodded. "Yes."

"When we get back, I'll give you the grand tour." Edna dipped through the door of the Tough Nickel as Dottie held the door with the toe of her shoe, a lit cigarette in one hand.

A strange chill brushed against my skin again, a contrast to the sunny day and the warmth I was feeling. I shivered and hoped it was just a trick of the wind then rushed past Dottie, dodging the smoke trailing from her mouth.

The Tough Nickel was honestly its own world. The shop sat snugly between two other cottage houses, but there was nothing ordinary about it. It was like an eccentric artist had poured all their creativity into one small space, resulting in a colorful, chaotic masterpiece.

The exterior of the shop was painted a bold, cheerful blue, which contrasted beautifully with the traditional white picket fence around it. A variety of objects were displayed in the windows—everything from an antique gramophone to a vintage mannequin wearing a striking sixties dress. Above the entrance, the name of the shop was painted in whimsical, curly letters, inviting everyone who passed by to explore its treasures.

A chorus of excited gasps filled the air once we all were inside. All but Dottie.

"We've died and gone to heavens, ladies." Charlie sighed as they all went on their separate ways through the thrift shop.

Inside, the Tough Nickel was a paradise of secondhand wonders. The air smelled of old books and the faint hint of well-loved clothing, a scent that promised the thrill of a good find. Shelves brimming with trinkets, books, clothing, and odds and ends lined the walls, while tables piled high with all sorts of items filled the spaces between. Each corner of the shop revealed a different treasure—a stack of old vinyl records, a selection of vintage cameras, a basket full of scarves in every color imaginable.

The Camping Cowgirls were immediately swept up in the enthusiasm of the place. Their eyes sparkled with excitement, each one eager to find her own treasure among the seemingly endless collection of goods. Some of them headed straight for the clothing racks, while others started rummaging through the pile of old board games.

Buck and Etta were standing at the counter when I approached. I couldn't help but notice the gorgeous pins Etta had laid out for Buck to assess.

"These are vintage brooches." Etta lightly touched one of them.

The ladies explored with the enthusiasm of kids in a candy store, leaving me some time to visit with Buck and Etta.

Laughter and delighted gasps filled the shop as they discovered one item after another. As I watched them, I couldn't help but feel a sense of contentment. There was something magical about the Tough Nickel—it was a place where the discarded was cherished, where the old was made new again.

"This one is, well, I just can't explain it." I pointed to one of Etta's brooches, in particular, that'd caught my eye. It was a vintage piece, possibly from the 1940s, its style harkening back to a time of glamour and elegance. I'd been to so many dress-up parties when I lived in New York City that I could identify pieces of jewelry from different eras pretty quickly.

The brooch was crafted in the shape of a peacock, its tail fanned out in an extravagant display. The body of the bird was made from polished silver, a testament to the craftsmanship of its era, and its tail was set with a multitude of small, shimmering stones. In the vibrant mix were aquamarines and sapphires, their hues ranging from the softest sky blue to the deepest midnight. When light hit the stones, they danced with a brilliance that was truly breathtaking.

The eye of the peacock was a single, radiant ruby, a perfect contrast to the cool tones of the tail feathers. Despite the age of the piece, the ruby's fiery glow hadn't dimmed one bit, its sparkle as captivating as ever.

Etta's peacock brooch wasn't just a piece of jewelry; it was a tiny work of art, a relic from a bygone era. You could almost feel the history emanating from it, a tangible link to the past and the stories it held.

"You know what? I think I'll keep that one." Etta picked it up and clipped it on her shirt. "It has special meaning."

A few of the Camping Cowgirls came up and were eyeballing Etta's treasures, picking them up faster than Buck could talk to Etta about them.

"Y'all should've seen the amazing things she has at her house." Dottie had come inside to join us. "Etta, are you gonna be taking part in the 127 Yard Sale tomorrow?"

"Of course I am." Etta then took it a step further, saying, "If you ladies think these things are golden gems, you need to stop by my house tomorrow. I'm actually going to open up an hour before the start time."

The women looked at each other with wide eyes, as if they were telepathically communicating to one another that they were for sure going to go to Etta's.

"I know her address, and I can give it to you tonight," I told them, then confided to Etta that the women were staying at Happy Trails Campground.

"That's where I got my lawn chair!" Dottie pointed at Etta. "They were asking me about it."

"Ah, I remember that old thing," Etta began, her sea-green eyes twinkling with a kind of fond reminiscence. "That one was a real piece of history, I tell ya."

She gestured with her weathered hands, fingers tracing the invisible outline of a chair that had long since left her possession. Her floral blouse caught the light above the counter and shimmered, as vibrant as the story she was about to spin.

"I'd picked it up myself from an estate sale down in Lebanon. The house it came from... Oh, it was grander than anything you'd ever seen. Old Southern charm just pouring out of every brick."

Her gaze grew distant, as though she was seeing not the crowd now gathered around her but the bygone days she was about to bring back to life in her story.

"That lawn chair had belonged to the matriarch of the family, a woman named Clara. She was a tough old bird, known throughout the county for her wit and her moonshine." The story garnered some oohs and aahs from the Camping Cowgirls. Even Fifi was still paying attention to Etta.

Mesmerized.

All of them.

"That chair was her throne. She'd sit on her porch every evening, watching the world go by, a jar of her moonshine in hand." Etta chuckled, a low, throaty sound that was as warm as the sun. "Why, she even had her initials carved into the backrest. C.B.: Clara Benson. She was quite a character. You've got a piece of history with that rocker. And I reckon it's found the right home with you, Dottie."

There was a sense of satisfaction in her voice, a junker's joy in seeing a discarded piece find a new purpose. I couldn't help but smile back, knowing the lawn chair would be more than just a chair to Dottie now. It was a tangible piece of a story, one that had started long before it came into our lives and one that would continue long after.

"Are you ladies ready?" Betts called from the door of the Tough Nickel. "The church needs their bus back tonight."

CHAPTER FOUR

Dottie and I had a lot to do when we got the Camping Cowgirls back to Happy Trails. Unfortunately, Dottie took a load off by sitting in her new-to-her lawn chair while I took care of all the to-dos for the Camping Cowgirls' first night.

The group had paid for all the extras. That included a fun night of s'mores by the large community campfire near the tiki hut, a little more toward the lake. It was a gorgeous gazebo, round and large enough for four full-sized swings that would fit three adults each, four if they were small enough.

Luckily for me, the group had decided to go junking for a few hours until it was time for them to come back for the campfire s'mores. Henry and Beck had already refilled all of the campers' woodpiles at each campsite. Each campsite also got its own s'mores starter kit, but they'd set up an entire cart filled with s'mores fixin's next to the gazebo as well.

As night fell and all the little details of their event came together, Happy Trails Campground transformed into a realm of twinkling magic. The string lights that hung between the trees turned on, casting a soft, ethereal glow over the area. It was a sight to behold, each tiny light a star that had descended to Earth, creating a constellation of our very own.

The vintage campers of the Camping Cowgirls added to the magical panorama of the campground. Each one was a glowing capsule of nostalgia, their windows spilling warm light onto the grass. They stood like beacons, their distinctive silhouettes a testament to the craftsmanship of bygone eras.

"Darn, Mae, look at them campers," Dottie murmured as we strolled toward the gazebo. Her Southern drawl danced over the words, the twang as comfortable as a well-worn quilt. "Ain't they just the cutest things you ever did see?"

I chuckled, following her gaze to the row of vintage campers, glowing like lanterns against the dark curtain of the night. I had to agree; there was a quaint charm about them that tugged at the corners of my heart.

Each camper had its own personality. Some were sleek and shiny, their polished metal bodies reflecting the twinkling lights hanging above. Others had been painted in vibrant hues, their colors a cheerful contrast to the quiet darkness around them.

Decorations added to the charm of each little home. Strings of fairy lights hung from awnings, draped over outdoor tables, or wound around nearby trees. The lights cast a soft glow onto the variety of lawn chairs, vintage coolers, and portable radios, imbuing each mundane item with a touch of enchantment.

There were outdoor rugs with bright, geometric patterns, inflatable flamingos standing sentinel, and colorful banners fluttering in the night breeze. Each site was a testament to the personality of its inhabitant, showcasing their flair for color, kitsch, or vintage charm.

The sight of these cozy campers, snug in their little nooks among the trees, was a comforting reminder of the group's shared love of adventure and friendship.

"I remember when I was a kid," Dottie continued, her eyes gleaming with fond nostalgia under the string lights. "We'd play house in them beat-up trailers down by Old Man Barger's lot. Seeing what they could've looked like, all spruced-up and shiny like something out of a picture book, makes me sad they sat down there and rotted."

Her words painted a vivid image in my mind, and I found myself lost in her memory of simpler days, when a rusted old trailer could be a castle, a spaceship, or a secret clubhouse.

"I reckon it's not just the campers, Dottie," I finally responded, my voice soft in the serenity of the night. "It's the folks inside 'em too. The Camping Cowgirls have certainly added a touch of magic to their places."

Dottie nodded, her eyes reflecting the twinkling lights from the campers. "You got that right, Mae. Just goes to show that one woman's junk is another woman's treasure."

"Yes. You've said that a million times today." I let go of a heavy sigh.

As we neared the gazebo, the aroma of roasting marshmallows wafted through the air, mingling with the scent of pine and campfire. The sound of laughter, soft conversations, and the soundtrack of the night was a soothing lullaby of nature's own making. The crackling fire added a comforting rhythm, the occasional pops and hisses like whispers in the dark. Nighttime critters began their chorus, a symphony of hoots, chirps, and rustling that ebbed and flowed with the wind.

The lake added its voice to the nocturnal harmony, each wave lapping gently against the shore. The distant crunch of leaves and the occasional snap of a branch reminded us of the wild expanse just beyond the tree line behind the campground, a world alive and vibrant under the moon's silver gaze.

The Camping Cowgirls sat around the campfire, the firelight dancing in their excited eyes. The day's adventures had left them with a wealth of stories and laughter. Their earlier enthusiasm had transformed into a sense of contentment, the satisfaction of a day well spent.

Charlie, her face illuminated by the warm glow of the fire, began to share an anecdote from their impromptu junking spree.

"Y'all should've seen Edna," she said, her voice filled with mirth. "She spotted this vintage necklace at one of the vendors. A real pretty thing, it was. But you know Edna—she's got a nose for a bargain."

Everyone nodded, smiles playing on their faces as they awaited the punch line. Dottie and I sat back and listened, just spectators until we were comfortable enough to know they didn't need us to hang with them.

"Well," Charlie continued, "she starts haggling with the poor guy. Telling him about the time she found a similar piece for half the price and how she couldn't possibly pay more than that. The guy was so flabbergasted, he agreed just to get her to stop."

Laughter erupted around the fire, each of them imagining the scene.

"Only Edna," someone said through their laughter, and we all nodded, our shared mirth echoing into the silver-tinted night.

As the laughter subsided, we settled into a comfortable silence, each of us lost in our thoughts under the starry sky.

Edna broke the silence. "I've got a campfire story."

As we all settled around the crackling fire, marshmallows roasting, the air rich with the scent of burnt sugar, Edna began her tale. The firelight painted her face with an eerie glow as she leaned in closer, her eyes sparkling with a mischievous glint.

"Years ago," she began, her voice low and laced with suspense, "there was a lady named Miss Evelyn who ran the pawnshop right here in Normal. She was known for her keen eye for valuable things, especially jewelry."

I settled in, a bag of marshmallows in my lap, riveted by Edna's tale. I had to admit, she had a knack for storytelling, and I wondered how many crime novels she'd devoured in her tenure as a librarian.

"Now, one day," Edna continued, "a handsome stranger walked into her shop with a piece of jewelry. An antique brooch, just as exquisite as the one Etta showed us today."

She painted a vivid picture of the brooch: a golden peacock with jeweled tail feathers and an eye made of a large, gleaming sapphire. But there was something unsettling about it.

"Miss Evelyn couldn't resist it, so she bought it," Edna said, her voice dropping a notch. "But soon, strange things started happening."

Listening to Edna's tale, I felt the familiar sight of the campground take on a more mysterious aspect. The shadows cast by the fire seemed to dance with a newfound intensity, and the occasional hoot of an owl in the distance sent a chill up my spine.

"Every time someone showed interest in the brooch, they'd disappear, leaving behind only their personal belongings. And the brooch, of course, would always find its way back to the pawnshop."

Edna paused, letting the tension of her story sink in. A collective shiver ran through the group. I looked around at the vintage campers and the tranquil lake, all bathed in a soft, moonlit glow. It was hard to imagine such eerie happenings in our peaceful town.

"Nobody knows what happened to those people or why the brooch caused such calamities. Miss Evelyn never sold it again, of course, but kept it hidden. Some say it's still somewhere in Normal, lying forgotten in a dusty old box."

The story ended, leaving a thrilling chill hanging in the air. I had to admit, Edna had a way of bringing even the most unnerving tales to life. I glanced around at the others, all wide-eyed and captivated, and couldn't suppress a shiver.

It's just a story, I reminded myself, though I had a feeling that tonight's shadows might seem just a bit deeper.

"I'm whooped." Dottie yawned, an unlit cigarette bouncing up and down in the corner of her mouth, her arms in the air, elbows fully extended.

"That's our signal that we've got a full day tomorrow, and we will leave you ladies to have the rest of these." I got up from the swing and put the bag of marshmallows on the cart as we all said goodnight.

"What's on the docket for tomorrow?" Dottie asked on our way across the campground, walking toward her camper.

"You're in the office while I go to church and spend the day getting a facial and haircut at the Cute-icles event," I reminded her. She opened her mouth but I kept talking before she could say anything. "You said you didn't want to go, and you didn't mind staying here."

"That was before I got my comfy lawn chair." Her face glowed as she brought her lighter's flame up to the end of her cigarette, sucking in as it came to life.

"After I get back, it's the place-setting contest that night under the awning of the recreational building. The Normal Diner is catering." I couldn't wait to see what Charlie had written down as their theme for the second night. I'd never seen a plate-themed supper, so my anticipation was high.

For the third night, they'd hired Blue Ethel and the Adolescent Farm Boys to play while Queenie French taught line dancing. I never knew Queenie did line dancing, much less taught it, but she claimed it was no different than teaching Jazzercise.

Either way, I was ready for it and willing to participate.

The women's voices carried across the lake, and I couldn't stop smiling. The closer I got to my camper van, the more memories of me and the Laundry Club Ladies fixing up this campground made me nostalgic, helping me see our future in these women.

However, my trip down Memory Lane didn't last too long.

Fifi was dancing around and letting out little yips from inside the camper van, waiting for me to take her out on her last nightly walk.

"Are you ready to go potty?" I opened the door. "Sit," I told her and reached into the camper to grab the basket with her leash. "You know you can't come outside all by yourself at night."

"Hey there, pretty lady!" I hadn't even heard Hank driving up, my mind still wrapped up in the day and being with the group of friends. "Can Chester and I join you?"

"Of course," I said, clipping on Fifi's leash and turning back around to see Hank in the middle of the campground road in his big truck, the window rolled down. "I'll meet you down there."

I let Fifi down after Hank started to drive off, or she would have been tugging me over to get into his truck. She loved him just as much as I did.

As the last echoes of laughter from s'mores night died away, Fifi and I waited for Hank and Chester to come out of their fifth wheel. Their home was three times as big as mine. It was a source of contention for us. I wanted to stay in my camper van once we were married, and he wanted to stay in his fifth wheel. His mama and Mary Elizabeth wanted us to move to a neighborhood where normal married people lived, according to them.

To us, normal married people lived in their camper.

If we could overcome our differing ideas about children, then we could surely overcome a little disagreement about which camper we would live in after we got hitched.

"How was your day?" Hank asked as soon as he opened the door and let Chester run out. Chester had spent most of his life as a hunting dog, so he had a keen sense of danger, unlike Fifi. Fifi tried like heck to run with Chester, but first I had to greet Hank properly.

With a kiss.

"I missed you today. We didn't get to talk much," he said and bent down to kiss me again. "We have a case—a missing teen. Jerry told the mom that all the leads we've gotten point to her daughter running away, but she insists we follow up on all the information and leads. It's her money."

"I'm sorry. I know it's frustrating." I looked into his eyes and could see a happy future with him, talking to him every night about what happened during each day. "But I know you'll find the teen, and she can tell her mom why she ran away."

"Yeah. I want a case with real meat. I'm starting to get antsy." Hank took my free hand and the leash from me, so Fifi could walk on his side.

"Are you considering going back into law enforcement?" I asked, knowing he'd left many different positions that involved carrying a badge. Many times, I'd questioned whether or not he would be happy being a private investigator, but I'd kept my mouth shut. It was his life, and I just wanted him to be happy.

"Nah. I think things need to stay the same until after we get married." He brought my beringed hand up to his lips and kissed the back. "Gosh. This is the kind of day that I'd love to end with a night in your arms."

"Just a few more months." I loved how he loved me. It'd been a long journey, but it was well worth every single good moment and bad moment we'd had.

"I see the Camping Cowgirls are all tucked in." Hank and I had rounded the far end of the lake and started up the side where the vintage campers were all lined up.

"They sure have." I didn't want to spoil the walk by telling him about the one thing still playing in my mind.

Edna's campfire story.

"It's a gorgeous evening." Hank continued to talk, his words intermingling with the soft rustle of leaves and the distant hoot of an owl. I had to admit I wasn't really listening. I was thinking about Edna's tale and how it had added a tinge of mystery to the night that I hadn't anticipated.

We strolled past the rows of vintage campers, each a charming pocket of warmth and light against the expansive backdrop of the Daniel Boone National Forest. The nostalgia of the day, mixed with the lingering effect of Edna's story, made the ordinary seem a little extraordinary.

Fifi, oblivious to my musings, pranced ahead, leash taut, her little tail wagging with joy as she tried to keep up with Chester on our moonlit adventure.

As we neared Edna's old Airstream, I noticed a figure behind the window. It was Edna, staring out at the night, a silhouette backlit by the soft glow from inside the camper.

Our eyes met, and for a moment, something flickered in her gaze that sent a chill down my spine. It was a look I couldn't quite place—a mix of fear, maybe, or excitement. But as quickly as it appeared, it was gone. Without a word, she pulled the shades down, the camper returning to an inscrutable, glowing sphere.

"Who is that?" Hank asked as if he could sense something.

"Edna Lee, one of the campers and a retired librarian." I rattled off the facts I knew about her.

As we walked past her Airstream, I couldn't shake off that strange moment. I looked back at the Bubble, its shiny surface reflecting the twinkling lights from the trees. A shiver ran down my spine, an echo of the thrill from the campfire story.

Maybe it was just my imagination, fueled by Edna's tale and the magic of the night. But I decided then, under the star-studded canopy of the forest, that I would keep an eye on Edna during her stay here. There was just something about her that didn't sit right in my gut.

"Did you hear what I said?" Hank stopped walking as soon as we passed Edna's camper.

"Yes. I answered you. Edna Lee," I said.

Hank took my hand and led me down to the beach. As we stepped upon the small dock to walk down the pier, he said, "I asked you about the wedding plans."

"You did?" My brows furrowed. My mind was so preoccupied with Edna and her odd behavior—at least, odd to me—that I'd not been present with the person I should be focusing on. "I'm so sorry. I've got a lot on my mind."

We reached the edge of the small pier, and Hank sat down. He patted the space next to him, and Fifi immediately took the spot. "I don't think so, little lady," Hank told her and picked her up, placing her in his lap.

That didn't suit Chester. His nails clicked on the wooden planks as he barreled down the pier, sticking his nose between me and Hank.

"What's on your mind?" Hank asked, both of us leaning the opposite way to let Chester have some room to climb into my lap. "Is it the wedding?"

"No. Nothing like that. We—the campground—have worked so hard to get it ready for the Camping Cowgirls that I think I'm just tired. I look around and think of more ways we could've made it better."

I didn't tell him what I was really thinking because the truth was,

Edna hadn't done anything to warrant the way I felt. It was just a weird feeling, nothing for Hank to be worried about, so I turned the tables.

"Which reminds me." I changed the subject and laid my head on his shoulder, our feet dangling just above the water's edge. "What is going on with the missing teen?"

"It's got me stumped. I've used all my available feelers and contacts. It's like she just vanished. Even her friends, who I thought she'd taken off with, said they'd not seen her." By the way he sounded, I could tell he was bothered by this one.

The water of the lake lay before us like a shimmering canvas. It was around ten o'clock, and the night had spread its dark veil over the Daniel Boone National Forest, the water reflecting the glittering specks of stars overhead. The only sounds were the gentle lapping of water against the wooden planks and the occasional hoot of an owl from the dense thicket.

In the quiet, gentle ripples appeared on the lake's surface. The tiny disturbances came and went like ghostly whispers, indicating the presence of small fish biting at the water's surface. They were barely noticeable unless you were really paying attention, tiny wrinkles on an otherwise still surface, like someone constantly throwing tiny pebbles into the water.

With Fifi curled up in Hank's lap and Chester nestled in mine, we sat there, a bubble of tranquility amid the mysterious nightlife of the forest. The two pets seemed to enjoy the calm just as much as we did, their eyes half-closed in contentment. Every so often, Fifi would lift her head and stare at the water, perhaps at the tiny disturbances caused by the fish.

Watching those subtle movements in the moonlight felt surreal, almost like seeing the heartbeat of the lake itself. The water would shimmer as the fish bit at its surface, capturing the scarce light and playing with it, as if the lake was winking at us. It was one of those beautifully rare moments when nature sang its quiet lullaby, and we found ourselves privileged enough to listen.

Hank's silence began to feel heavier, laden with thoughts he was wrestling with. This case was gnawing at him in a way I'd never seen before.

"You okay, Hank?" I asked, breaking the silence. "I mean, really okay?"

Hank let out a sigh, a soft gust of air in the calm of the night. He glanced at me, his brows furrowed in that familiar way when a case had him stumped. "It's this case, Mae. The missing girl."

I nodded, my heart aching at the troubled look in his eyes.

"The leads, they're all... dead ends," he confessed, his voice filled with frustration. "It's like she just vanished into thin air. I told you I have exhausted all my contacts."

There was a note of desolation in his words that tugged at my heart. Hank was an excellent private investigator; he had a knack for connecting dots that others couldn't see. But this case seemed to be giving him a run for his money.

"I wish I had something more to go on," he said, looking out at the dark waters of the lake. "The parents are worried sick, Mae. I can't stand the idea of not finding her."

I reached out, gently squeezing his hand. "You're doing everything you can, Hank. No one could do more."

He nodded, though I could tell my words didn't entirely assuage his worry. The weight of the case was pressing on his broad shoulders.

We fell into silence again, each lost in our own thoughts. The case hung in the air between us like an unfinished puzzle, pieces missing, the image unclear. But as we sat there under the night sky, I knew Hank wouldn't rest until he'd turned every stone, chased every lead, and done everything in his power to bring that girl home.

I didn't know how this case would unravel, but one thing was certain. Hank was determined, and he wouldn't give up. Not until he had answers. The resolve in his eyes, illuminated by the soft glow of the moon, assured me of that.

"Enough of my thoughts." He shook his head and looked at me. His beautiful green eyes always seemed as if he were seeing me for the first time, like he had a few years ago in this very spot. "What's going on with the wedding?"

I sucked in a deep breath. "Tomorrow, you promised Mary Elizabeth we'd go to church with her. Then we have the undercroft luncheon before we go to Cute-icles for Helen Pyle's fun-filled spa day," I said, reminding him of what we'd signed up for months ago. "And tomorrow night is our couples counseling with Preacher Alex."

"Oh geesh. How on earth is the man going to counsel us when he's single? Never been married?"

Hank made me laugh at the irony. "You know Mary Elizabeth," I prompted him. "She would rather die than us not fulfill the marriage requirement."

It wasn't necessary to have pre-marriage counseling, but it was something that would make Mary Elizabeth so happy that an hour of our time wasn't going to hurt us. "It's just an hour." I rested my chin on his shoulder, looking at him.

"We won't need but five minutes with him."

Hank was so easygoing that I had no doubt he was right.

We sat there for about another half hour, the night gently folding around us. A peacefulness lay over the campground, under the watchful eyes of the twinkling stars.

CHAPTER FIVE

A hush fell over the church as Preacher Alex Elliott stepped behind the podium. Despite bearing the youthful countenance of a thirteen-year-old boy, there was an authority about him that commanded respect. His voice rang clear, reverberating in the high-ceilinged chapel, a welcome note on a fine Sunday morning.

"Good morning," he began, his gaze sweeping over the congregation. But then, it stilled, focused on a point somewhere near the front.

An inexplicable chill ran down my spine. His eyes seemed to lock onto something—or someone. I felt a strange urge to confirm my suspicions, and I stole a quick glance over my shoulder. The wooden pew creaked beneath me as I shifted, the noise hardly a whisper in the quiet.

I had barely moved when I felt it, that intense gaze on me. When I turned back, a sudden flush crept up my neck. The preacher's eyes, so young yet filled with a depth that belied his years, were on me.

Me.

For a moment, everything seemed to stop—the faint rustle of Sunday dresses, the soft murmur of reverence, even the echo of the preacher's own voice. All I could see were those eyes, staring, assessing, almost piercing me.

His gaze held me, and in that moment, I was the only one in the crowded room. The spotlight was on me, and for a heartbeat, it felt like I was the target of his sermon and he was delivering it directly to me.

The realization hit me like a summer thunderbolt. I was the subject of Preacher Alex Elliott's undivided attention, an unwavering focus that held me captive and shook me to the core.

A sudden, inexplicable knot formed in my throat, a strange mixture of surprise and unease. Almost instinctively, I attempted a discreet throat-clearing, hoping to diffuse the building tension. As if on cue, a soft touch landed on my leg, gentle but firm. *Mary Elizabeth.*

Her touch was comforting, a silent reassurance in the face of my unexpected discomfort. With the tenderness only a foster-adoptive mama could muster, she patted my leg as if telling me, "All is well." It was an intimate gesture, as soft and familiar as a well-loved quilt.

Her joy was contagious, lighting up her eyes with a warmth that matched the Sunday-morning sun. She sat tall in the pew, radiating a sort of pride that was impossible to ignore. To her right was Hank, his quiet strength a comforting presence, while I filled the spot on her left.

Mary Elizabeth looked like she'd struck gold, her face glowing with a happiness so pure it could've rivaled the sparkle of a lottery-jackpot winner. For her, the simple act of us flanking her in church was the grand prize, a winning ticket in the lottery of life. To an outsider, it might seem like an ordinary Sunday, but to Mary Elizabeth, it was a celebration. A celebration of us, of family, of moments that made the everyday extraordinary. And in the warm embrace of her joy, everything else felt inconsequential, even the unsettling gaze of Preacher Alex.

As the final hymn rang out, Mary Elizabeth's voice soared above the rest, a powerful, harmonious melody that enveloped the entire congregation. It was as if her joy had found a new channel, her voice a vibrant testament to the pure elation coursing through her. Her song was a beautiful symphony of devotion and happiness, and it filled the chapel with a tangible warmth that made the stained-glass windows seem to glow just a little brighter.

As her voice continued to echo in the lofty chapel, I found myself looking around. There they were, our friends and neighbors, their faces familiar and comforting in their Sunday best. Sunday was a day of ease in our little Southern town, a day when time seemed to slow down, when every second was savored and every moment cherished. It was a charm that our town held close, a charm that made it our own little piece of heaven on earth.

Eventually, the final notes of the hymn drifted into silence, replaced by the voice of Preacher Alex, his gaze no longer unsettling but somehow invigorating.

"Well, that's it for today," he announced, a warm smile breaking across his boyish face. "The Bible Thumper Church Bible Study Ladies have prepared a wonderful luncheon for us all in the undercroft. Let us continue our fellowship there."

He garnered a collected giggle from the congregation, making himself very likable because in truth, they weren't called the Bible Thumpers—it was just a name given to them around town, no different than the townspeople calling me and my friends the Laundry Club Ladies because we always congregated at Betts's laundromat.

And with that, he dismissed the congregation. The chapel buzzed back to life as everyone began to stir, the end of the sermon signaling the start of another tradition in our charming little town—the Sunday luncheon, where friendships were strengthened, stories were shared, and our sense of community was celebrated. It was the perfect end to the Sunday service, the cherry on top of our slow and easy Southern Sundays.

All of us eventually made it down to the undercroft by way of going outside and around the building.

I glanced around. The sun even appeared to be happy as it set, as if it too were proud of the comfortable smiles, the unhurried chatter, the children running in their Sunday best on the grassy patch outside the chapel. It was as if the whole town took a collective breath on Sundays, the day unfolding like a sweet, lazy summer dream.

The earthy scent of the old basement mingled with the mouthwatering aroma of home-cooked food. The undercroft was just a large room, a vast open space with a kitchen tucked behind a pass-through counter. It was expansive enough for Queenie's daily Jazzercise classes, but today, the room had transformed.

Rows of banquet tables filled the area, the usual echoes of jazz music replaced with the soft hum of conversation and laughter. The air buzzed with the cozy familiarity of communal meals and the excited chatter of friends and neighbors ricocheting off the old stone walls.

A sensory delight unfolded before me as the Bible Thumpers navigated through the bustling crowd to put plates of food in front of everyone who stayed for the luncheon. The plates held mountains of comfort food: fried chicken that crackled under your teeth before giving way to succulent meat, mashed potatoes creamy and warm, and green beans cooked to perfection with a slight crunch.

And the biscuits.

Oh, the biscuits. Their scent wafted through the undercroft, a familiar and comforting aroma that felt like a warm embrace. I took a bite, the flaky exterior giving way to a warm, buttery interior. It was pure bliss—the kind of taste that had you closing your eyes to savor every morsel. They were the best Southern biscuits you'd ever tasted, and I could say that with absolute certainty.

Because these weren't just any biscuits. They were Mary Elizabeth's contributions, each one kneaded, rolled, and baked with the same love and care she'd always shown me. And every bite, every taste, was a testament to the love that she and this charming little town brimmed with.

"Mae!" The playful exclamation from Bobby Ray, my foster brother, pulled me from my thoughts. His fingers snapped audibly in front of my face, the sharp sound echoing around us. "Earth to Mae! Could you pass the honey?" His finger pointed insistently.

With a smile, I reached for the bottle and passed it across the table to where he and Abby sat, absorbed in their own world.

Hank's hand came down gently on my back, the contact grounding me in reality. "She's been in her own head this morning," he divulged, his voice laced with concern. "I think she's anxious about the marriage counseling session with Preacher Alex tonight."

"Nonsense." Abby chimed in, her voice a soothing melody. She nudged Bobby Ray, who was drizzling a veritable avalanche of honey onto his biscuit. "We were in and out in a matter of minutes."

"But you didn't have Preacher Alex staring at you throughout the service," I countered, remembering the intense, peculiar gaze that had unsettled me during the sermon.

"That's only because we aren't regulars here." Queenie's fingers deftly pushed back the sparkly headband that threatened to slip off her short, blond hair. She was never seen without a headband, but for today, she'd traded her usual Jazzercise gear for a fetching sundress.

"Maybe you should consider becoming regulars. It was nice having you all here," Betts interjected, her voice imbued with her signature warmth.

"I must admit, this meal is scrumptious." I took another bite of my own biscuit, its buttery goodness melting in my mouth. "Thanks, Betts. This gathering means a lot to the community."

"And don't forget about our Wednesday spaghetti supper." Betts didn't miss a beat, her eyes twinkling with delight. "And, of course, we've always got room for more in the Bible Thumpers."

It was no secret Betts wanted us to join, but with the countless obligations like visiting the prison and counseling the inmates, I just wasn't ready to commit.

Suddenly, Hank's question sliced through my thoughts. "Where's Ryan?" He wiped his mouth with a napkin and placed it atop his empty plate, Bobby Ray following suit.

Before we could blink, one of the Bible Thumpers had cleared their plates, replacing them with slices of mouth-watering Kentucky Derby Pie.

"Ryan's on frying duty," Betts informed us, a wry smile playing on her lips as she looked toward the kitchen. Ryan had somehow found himself volunteering in the church kitchen, despite not being an official church member.

Yet.

Just as I was about to take a bite of my Kentucky Derby Pie, a boisterous laugh echoed through the undercroft. I didn't need to turn around to know it was Dottie. Her infectious laughter was as distinct as her colorful Southern sayings.

"Well, I'll be," Dottie began, her Southern accent drawing out each syllable. "If I had known y'all serve such fine pie at church, I would've found religion a long time ago!" Her comment was followed by another burst of hearty laughter, causing everyone around the table to chuckle.

Dottie, wearing her usual eye-catching ensemble of a Hawaiian shirt and pink flamingo earrings, leaned back in her chair, patting her belly with satisfaction. "I swear, this pie is so good, it's like I've died and gone to heaven. But don't you worry, Lord. I ain't ready to meet you just yet. Not before I've had another slice of this divine creation!"

Her statement brought another round of laughter. Betts, shaking her head in amusement, handed Dottie a second slice of pie. "Well, Dottie, we wouldn't want to deprive you of any heavenly experiences. Here you go."

Laughter and lighthearted chatter filled the undercroft, our little group becoming the life of the party. With friends like these, who wouldn't feel blessed?

As everyone at the tables continued to devour the delicious Southern delicacies, I heard an unmistakable sound, a crackling voice that made my heart lurch. It was the squawk of Hank's police scanner, a device he stubbornly refused to part ways with even after leaving the force—a reminder of his past and a tether to the world he once served.

The familiar hum of the scanner seemed alien amidst the cheerful banter and clinking cutlery. Betts, Abby, Dottie, Queenie, and I all instinctively swiveled in our seats toward the source. We listened to the police scanner every day down at the laundromat.

Hank, his brows furrowed, pulled the compact device from his pocket and held it up to his ear.

"What's the buzz, Hank?" I asked, my heart pounding.

His confusion was palpable, his gaze distant.

"Is it your missing teen case?" I tried to keep my voice steady, even though my mind was racing with all sorts of horrible scenarios.

The silence that followed felt as heavy as a church bell. "No... It's Etta Hardgrove. She's... She's dead." His voice was somber, the words lingering in the air like an ominous fog.

Dottie was the first to break the silence. "Well, ain't that a kick in the pants!" She sprang to her feet, her hand snatching her cigarette case and the remaining slice of pie from the table. "No rest for the wicked, ladies!"

"Where are y'all going?" Mary Elizabeth asked. "What about our spa afternoon?"

A pang of guilt sliced through me as I looked at Mary Elizabeth's expectant face. She'd been looking forward to our spa afternoon, a rare moment of tranquility in our typically chaotic lives. But circumstances had taken a sharp, unexpected turn.

"We've got a bit of a situation, Mary Elizabeth," I called over my shoulder, cringing slightly at the disappointment that flickered in her eyes. "Etta Hardgrove... She's... Well, she's passed."

"Etta?" Her face paled, her hand moving instinctively to her heart. "Oh, mercy."

"I'm sorry, Mary Elizabeth," I said, my own heart aching. "We just need to check things out. Spa day will have to wait."

"But," she stammered, her Southern charm momentarily shattered by the tragic news, "Etta was just fine this morning in Sunday school. She was..."

"Talking about that brooch," Dottie interrupted, her usually jovial tone replaced with something far more somber. "I overheard her before she walked out the door. You remember, the one she was showing off to the Camping Cowgirls."

I saw recognition flash in Mary Elizabeth's eyes. "Oh, dear Lord, you don't think..."

"We don't know yet," I replied, shaking my head. "But we intend to find out."

Within moments, we were in motion, a small whirlwind of urgency.

The other Laundry Club Ladies piled into Betts's van, their faces a cocktail of shock, disbelief, and determination. Hank and I, meanwhile, bolted to his truck.

As we pulled away from the undercroft, I cast a glance over my shoulder. Mary Elizabeth stood there, her figure shrinking in the rearview mirror. Her hands were clasped as though in prayer, and I felt a shiver run down my spine. This mystery was just beginning, and something told me it was going to be anything but straightforward.

CHAPTER SIX

As we rounded the corner, Etta's house came into view. A charming old cottage, it was cluttered with an assortment of items she had collected over the years, now laid out on her lawn for the 127 Yard Sale. The grass was trampled from the foot traffic of countless bargain hunters, creating an eerie contrast to the jubilant chaos that had consumed it just yesterday morning during Etta's curb alert. The sight stirred a pang of nostalgia within me, a harsh reminder of how swiftly circumstances could change.

Sheriff Al Hemmer was there, bumbling about in his brown sheriff's uniform, his deputies scrambling to keep up with his aimless directions. Al had the heart for law enforcement, bless him, but lacked the tact and precision needed in delicate situations.

Ranger Tucker Pyle was also there, towering over everyone else. He was a man of the forest, more at home in the sprawling canopy of the Daniel Boone National Forest than in a suburban setting. He looked as out of place as a deer in a china shop, yet his eyes were sharp and focused, taking in every detail with calculated precision. The only reason Tucker was here was because this part of the forest was in his district. It was one of his duties. If the sheriff's department could handle the situation, then Tucker would step aside. But from the looks of Al, I wasn't sure he was going to be able to handle anything.

Just on the outskirts of the scene, lurking like a vulture around a carcass, was Waldo Willy. With his intrusive camera and his notebook always at the ready, he was Normal's resident newshound. As quick to find drama as a bloodhound on a scent, he was already angling for photos and statements, weaving through the scene with an ease that surpassed even Al's deputies.

Hank pulled into Etta's driveway, the tires crunching over the gravel. Our arrival attracted Waldo's attention, and he made a beeline toward us, camera snapping. Ignoring him, the Laundry Club Ladies piled out of the van, and we got out of the truck, our senses assailed by the scene that lay before us.

Etta's home, once a haven of eccentric charm, was now a crime scene. A stark, cold reality set in. The little town of Normal, it seemed, was anything but.

Hank dismissed himself. "I'll go see what happened to her."

As soon as Hank walked away, Waldo walked up. His thick glasses magnified his eager eyes, and his notepad was poised in his hand like a weapon. His camera hung around his neck, occasionally being lifted for an indiscreet snap.

"Laundry Club Ladies, mind giving a statement?" He trotted alongside us, his short legs working twice as hard to keep up with our long strides. "Dottie, what do you make of this sudden turn of events?"

He aimed his camera up at Dottie, who didn't even break her stride as she responded with a sharp, "Waldo, you're on us like ants on a dropped lollipop."

Undeterred, Waldo bobbed around us like an overeager puppy, trying to get his scoop. "Betts, any insight you might want to share? Abby, what's your take on all this? Queenie, do you think this might affect your Jazzercise classes?"

We exchanged glances, suppressing smirks. Poor Waldo. The boy just didn't know when to quit.

"Sorry, Waldo," I finally told him, offering a polite smile. "But we've got no comments for you at the moment."

He huffed a little, seeming disappointed but not surprised. He was persistent, I'd give him that. He nodded, scribbled something down, then, with a parting shot from his camera, scurried off to bother someone else.

As I stood there, my eyes were drawn to the flurry of activity around Etta's quaint cottage-style house. The official vehicles were parked haphazardly, their lights flashing silently. It felt surreal, a ripple in the smooth surface of our otherwise serene town.

From where I was, I could see Hank in the middle of a group that included Al, Tucker, and a couple of deputies. They were talking, their expressions grave. Hank's gaze met mine briefly before he pulled out his phone, excusing himself from the group to answer a call. His brows furrowed in concentration as he listened to whoever was on the other end.

Curiosity had my heart racing, but I forced myself to wait. When he finally ended the call and strode over to me, his expression was a mix of frustration and hope. "Mae," he began, rubbing his temple, "I just got a lead on the missing teenager. They think she might be in Slade."

The seriousness in his voice instantly drained my curiosity. "Do you need to leave now?" I asked.

He nodded. "If it's all right with you, I can ask Betts to give you a lift home."

I assured him it was okay, and with a quick, concerned kiss on my forehead, he was off, leaving me to watch the spectacle unfold. It was then that I saw it—Colonel Holz's black hearse pulling up. My breath hitched as I saw the men bring out a gurney with a body bag, and that's when it hit me. Etta was really gone.

From my vantage point, I overheard snippets of their conversation. "Suspect," "crime scene," "head wound." The words hung heavily in the air.

"Did you hear that?" Dottie was by my side, her eyes wide with anticipation. "They said 'head wound.' And 'suspects'! Do you think Etta was... murdered?"

I couldn't help but shiver at the implication. Something told me that life in Normal was about to get a lot less normal.

A familiar dread filled my stomach. Poor Etta. She had been full of life, stories, and amazing brooches. And now...

My thoughts were interrupted when I heard another fragment of conversation from the huddle of law enforcement officials. "Looks like a struggle." Something about that phrase made me shudder. Etta had certainly been full of fight, but it looked like someone had fought back.

"We don't know anything yet," I said, trying to comfort Dottie.

That didn't work. She snapped open her pleather cigarette case, where she batted out a smoke and lit it. She puffed so hard, the end of it lit up like the color of her hair. With one of her arms curled around her waist, she shifted on her left hip and watched the scene through the plumes of smoke curling around her head.

Turning from the crime scene, I noticed Betts, Abby, and Queenie engaged in conversation with a small crowd that had gathered nearby. The faces of the newcomers were a mix of shock and morbid curiosity. Perhaps they were potential customers who'd come for Etta's much-anticipated 127 Yard Sale spread. Who knew they'd end up at a crime scene instead?

I could see each one of my friends navigating the crowd with practiced ease, their Southern charm turned on full blast. They were skilled at blending into any situation, their genuine warmth drawing people in and making them feel comfortable enough to open up. Right now, they were doing what they did best—extracting tidbits of information from the locals.

As I made my way toward them, I couldn't help but feel a pang of concern. *What if someone among this crowd is responsible for Etta's death?* It was a chilling thought, but we were living in a chilling reality.

Betts was deep in conversation with an older gentleman in a faded flannel shirt with some garage-sale pieces in his arms, while Queenie and Abby were talking animatedly to a group of young women who looked like they'd come straight from a yoga class. I noted their eagerness to contribute, to help in any way they could. It was a testament to the tight-knit community we lived in—a community that had just lost one of its members.

Despite the grim circumstances, I was proud of how everyone was pulling together. This was Normal, after all—a small town where everyone looked out for one another. And as I watched my friends work the crowd, gathering information, I knew we were going to get to the bottom of this.

For Etta.

Betts, Abby, and Queenie reconvened with me, their eyes sparkling with the thrill of their impromptu fact-finding mission. I noticed a solemn determination in their faces. We were all feeling the weight of the situation.

"Dottie looks pretty upset," Abby said.

"We just talked to Etta yesterday." I held up two fingers. "Twice." I quickly told them about how we'd showed up for the curb alert and then saw her again at the Tough Nickel.

"I spoke to a fella named Pete, runs a local farmstead just past the highway," Betts began, her voice hushed. "Said he'd come down early for the yard sale. Saw Etta just this morning, fit as a fiddle. She'd even bargained with him over a set of porcelain roosters."

The idea of Etta alive and haggling only a few hours ago sent a pang of sadness through me. This had been her town, her life, and it had all abruptly ended.

Abby piped up next, her arms crossed over her chest. "Those girls we were talking to? They do sunrise yoga in the park nearby." Abby and Queenie both pointed to a little neighborhood park across the street. "Said they'd seen Etta fussing with a woman in the early hours."

Queenie chimed in, her blond hair bobbing as she nodded along. "Sure did. They said the woman had a brooch that caught the light, and we all know Edna's fondness for those."

A shiver rippled down my spine. This couldn't be a coincidence. But I stayed quiet.

Abby chewed on her lower lip, a sign of deep thought, her usually sparkling eyes taking on a more serious look. Finally, she took a deep breath and began to speak. "The woman Etta talked to? Silver-haired, tallish, slender frame. Age spots on her hands, which they noticed because she was gesturing a lot," Abby explained, her gaze distant as she relayed the yoga girls' description. "She was wearing this large, ornate brooch, a dragonfly or something, that glinted in the early-morning light. And, oh, her voice. They said it was a little high-pitched, the kind that carries. You know... the kind you can hear from across a crowded room."

She stopped, studying my face for a moment. My eyebrows knitted together as I connected the dots, too hesitant to voice my suspicion. Yet I knew whom she was talking about. The description was too specific, the details too coincidental.

The same chill I'd gotten yesterday was back. Only this time, it made me shiver. The description wasn't concrete proof, but it was enough to make us all consider the uncomfortable possibility that Edna might be involved in Etta's death.

Clad in its ranger uniform, Tucker's broad frame advanced toward me. His expression was serious, all furrowed brows and focused eyes, and with every deliberate step, his boots crunched on the gravel.

"Heard something intriguing about yoga girls," Tucker said, a slight questioning arch to his eyebrow that invited me to share more.

Taking in a deep breath, I narrated Abby's account, each detail pouring out of me like a suspense-filled narrative. Tucker's eyes, reminiscent of the calm blue lake, widened in quiet surprise. His thick fingers ran through his sun-bleached hair as he sighed. "Sheriff Hemmer ought to hear this." He motioned for me to follow him.

The crunch of Tucker's boots on the gravel rang out as we made our way toward the back of Etta's house. A subtle unease tightened around my heart, the gravity of the situation sinking deeper with each passing second.

Al Hemmer, ensnared within the veil of his professional duties, was hunched over Etta's lifeless body. Etta's face was a stark contrast to the lively and argumentative woman she was just yesterday. Now she lay still, a pitiful sight that sent cold shivers crawling down my spine.

Sheriff Hemmer, despite his clumsiness, was a transformed man on this job. He stood tall, his usual air of fumbling uncertainty replaced with a grave seriousness that fit the morbid scene.

Colonel Holz, the grizzled, no-nonsense coroner, stood alongside Al. His gnarled hands, steady despite the years, pointed toward Etta's head. "A severe blow to the head. That's what did her in," he muttered, the solemnity of his tone resonating through the quiet backyard. His words hung heavily in the air, casting a foreboding shadow over the entire gathering.

"Murder?" My question was barely a whisper, barely a hiccup in the gloomy quietude. But it felt like a shriek, like a scream that echoed the shock coursing through my veins.

"Murder," Al conceded, his eyes reflecting a flicker of the regret he must've felt for his loose tongue. "But never you mind." He tried to recover, but the horse had bolted from the stable. He groaned, slapping his forehead. "All right, out with it. What've you got?"

Gulping down the dryness in my throat, I recounted the story about the yoga girls and the suspicious woman, the one who bore an uncanny resemblance to Edna, a Happy Trails Campground guest with a group of traveling women called Camping Cowgirls.

As I recounted the puzzling information gathered from the yoga girls, Al looked deep in thought, his fingers drumming a silent rhythm against his stubbled chin. "That ain't a whole lot to go on, Mae. But if you want to snoop a little around this Edna, do it. Just... be careful. And otherwise, stay out of it," he warned, even though I knew he was really wanting me to keep an ear out for anything that would help.

Or at least, I took it that way.

He waved me off.

On my way back around the house to meet back up with the Laundry Club Ladies, my phone buzzed in my pocket, breaking me out of my thoughts.

It was Mary Elizabeth, her voice thick with theatrical disappointment. "Mae, honey, you're missing our Cute-icles appointment," she whined, an undercurrent of guilt wrapped around each word.

"All right, all right. I'm on my way." I sighed. I turned to Betts. "Can you drop me at the beauty parlor?"

Knowing there wasn't much more we could do standing here, we all piled into Betts's van, a little less chatty than usual.

As Betts drove off, I let my eyes wander over Etta's neighborhood. Each house was a charming replica of the next, with neatly manicured lawns and vibrantly colored blooms adorning the white picket fences. Across the street, children played in the neighborhood park while their parents were gathered on the curb, no doubt gossiping about what was going on over at Etta's house.

Amid all this beauty, the grim reality of Etta's death loomed heavily. This wasn't just a mystery to be solved—it was now a murder case. And somehow, I had a feeling we were just scratching the surface.

CHAPTER SEVEN

The pungent scents of perm solution and nail polish wafted through the lively buzz of Cute-icles, mingling with the comforting aroma of brewing coffee. Amidst the warm, heady smells, the playful clinks of metal hair shears echoed off the bubblegum-pink walls, joining the steady hum of the dryer hoods. The candy-colored row of nail polish bottles perched on a lacy doily-covered table twinkled under the fluorescent lights, a colorful collection ranging from mint green to soft lavender, fire-engine red to sunny yellow.

Emmalyn Truman, wife of Hank's partner Jerry, her eyes hidden under cotton pads soaked in cucumber water, reached out a hand delicately painted in lavender polish, her voice slicing through the chatter. "Mae," she began, her tone laden with urgency. "The boys ain't getting anywhere with that missing-teenager case. Do you reckon it is a runaway?"

While I pondered her words, I caught fragmented whispers of a conversation from the group of ladies by the waxing station. They murmured about the 127 Yard Sale, Etta's penchant for hoarding, and the lingering hint of a rumor about her husband wanting to leave her. I committed each snippet to memory, stowing them away for later perusal.

"Hoarding?" I asked, glancing over at Sally Ann.

Mary Elizabeth was seated in Sally Ann's domain, a flamboyant manicure station that was a riot of glittery nail files, buffing blocks, and cuticle trimmers. Sally Ann herself was blowing a bubble of pink gum while working her magic on Mary Elizabeth's nails, transforming them into glossy pink gems.

Sally Ann was holding court at the nail station, chewing the wad of gum in her mouth as she shaped Mary Elizabeth's nails. "Etta was actin' peculiar, I tell ya," she chimed in, tossing me a quick glance. Her voice, a singsong mixture of gossip and friendly banter, melded into the hum of the salon. "Sure actin' strange, wasn't she? And I heard from one of the college girls in here yesterday, Adrienne, that Etta's daughter told her Etta's marriage was in trouble. Can you imagine?"

"Her husband's name is Clay, right?" I asked, thinking this could be a motive for murder.

"Clay. Mm-hmm," Sally Ann hummed. "Why does that matter?" She frowned.

I couldn't answer, as I was getting my hair washed. The familiar scent of shampoo and conditioner wafted up my nostrils as Helen's fingers gently massaged my scalp, the sounds of running water providing a soothing background noise on a normal day—but today was not normal.

When she sat me up again, I said to Sally Ann, "I don't know. I guess I'm just curious."

"Do you think he did it?" she asked, her own cherry-red fingernails flitting like butterflies over Mary Elizabeth's hands. The click-clack of her nail file was a steady rhythm in the background.

Helen took the towel and started to run it through my hair, careful to avoid any rough handling that might lead to frizzing when it dried.

"I don't know. I didn't say that." I did my best to keep my tone casual. "Tell me more about what Adrienne said, Sally Ann."

Sally Ann paused in her filing and glanced over at me, a smug smile spreading across her face. "Well, now, Mae, you know it ain't polite to gossip," she drawled, her Southern twang as thick as the humidity outside. "But since you're asking..."

She lowered her voice, leaning in closer as though sharing a secret. "Adrienne was in here just yesterday, getting her nails done for the summer. She was chattin' away about Clay and Etta Hardgrove. She said Etta's daughter Jenna told her that Clay was fixin' to leave Etta."

A sudden hush fell over the salon, followed by a flurry of murmurs. I could see eyes growing wide in the mirrors and heads nodding. It seemed every corner of Cute-icles was a hotbed for gossip—be it the buzz beneath the helmet hair dryers, the whispered exchanges at the shampoo bowls, or the secretive conversations under the hot-wax stations.

"Leave her?" I repeated, trying to keep the surprise out of my voice.

"That's right. According to Jenna, their marriage has been on the rocks for some time now. Etta's hoarding got worse and worse after their kids moved out. Clay couldn't stand living with the mess any longer, Adrienne said. Apparently, he's been staying in a motel for the past few weeks."

The sharp tang of nail polish filled my nostrils as Sally Ann applied a glossy coat to Mary Elizabeth's nails. My mind whirled with this new information. Could Clay really have left Etta because of her hoarding? Could this be tied to Etta's sudden death?

"Well, that's certainly interesting, Sally Ann," I said, trying to hide the way my mind was racing. It seemed like every piece of information I learned about Etta Hardgrove just gave me more questions than answers.

Mary Elizabeth, however, was having none of it. "Ladies, we're here for a li'l R&R and a special spa day," she admonished, her sweet Southern drawl filling the space. "Helen, dear, how 'bout we try some hairstyles on Mae for her big day?"

"But the wedding isn't for another three months," I protested, only to be silenced by a stern glance from Mary Elizabeth.

She waved away my protest, her eyes twinkling with an excitement that could only be stirred by the prospect of wedding planning. "No harm in being prepared, darling. Helen, what about a French twist or some romantic curls?"

As Helen guided me over to a seat near the window for a quick trim, Emmalynn's voice rose above the hum of hair dryers and the subtle gossipy whispers. "You know," she said, her voice carrying with a surety only a cop's wife would have, "Etta was always putting those curb alerts in the *Gazette*. It's like an invitation to all sorts. You just never know who's going to crawl out of the woods for a free deal."

Helen snorted, a good-natured eye roll accompanying her action as she draped a cape over me and began combing through my damp hair. "Emmy, you make it sound like we're inviting criminals over for tea."

"Well, Helen, we might as well be with all those curb alerts. It doesn't look good for our town, now does it?" Emmalynn countered, a teasing twinkle in her eyes.

Mary Elizabeth, her nails now gleaming with a fresh coat of polish, chimed in. "Oh, Emmalyn, you do have a point. But it's Sheriff Al's job to keep us safe and solve this awful murder."

Over by the manicure station, Sally Ann had taken to applying a topcoat to Mary Elizabeth's nails. "I hope Al solves it soon," she said. "People are talking, you know."

Their banter filled the salon, their concerns echoing my own thoughts.

Gazing out the window at the bustling street, I took in the familiar sights of our small Southern town. Tourists still meandered about, oblivious to the undercurrent of unease that had settled amongst the locals.

I found myself lost in thought, ruminating over the clues. Edna, the woman Abby described, was a strong suspect. She had shown interest in the brooch Etta owned. But Clay... He had motive too. If what Adrienne said was accurate and he had been planning to leave Etta, did he decide to expedite the process?

My fingers tapped rhythmically on the armrest as I turned these thoughts over. I needed more evidence, more leads.

For now, though, I had to keep an open mind and stay vigilant. The conversation in the salon had given me a new perspective, and as I watched the familiar view of the town, I resolved to get to the bottom of this mystery. One way or another, I would uncover the truth behind Etta Hardgrove's death.

Helen, with nimble fingers and a concentrated look on her face, went to work on my curly mane, taming it into a smooth, sleek French twist. She pinned it in place, then turned me around to face the mirror.

"There," she said with a satisfied smile. "What do you think?"

I scrutinized my reflection, turning my head this way and that. My curls, usually wild and free, were now swept up and secured, leaving my neck and shoulders bare. It was sophisticated, sure, but it didn't feel like me.

"I don't know, Helen," I began, trying to choose my words carefully. "It just feels a bit... not me."

Just then, Mary Elizabeth, who had been watching the whole thing while blowing on her newly painted nails, burst into laughter. "Oh, Mae," she chuckled, "you've got to show off those shoulders while you can! You ain't getting any younger, honey. And let me tell you, when you have kids, well... they take a toll on you."

"You can get having kids right off the bat out of your head," I warned Mary Elizabeth.

Still, as I looked at my reflection again, the elegant twist of hair felt foreign. I wasn't ready to give up my wild curls just yet. I shook my head, my eyes meeting Helen's in the mirror.

"Let's try something else," I said politely to Helen, even though I didn't want to try anything. But I was here to spend some time with Mary Elizabeth, and I could take one for the team.

Emboldened by our laughter and the collaborative atmosphere, Helen decided to try something a bit more daring. "How about a high, bouncy ponytail? Something a bit youthful and playful?"

She worked my hair into a high ponytail that sat right at the crown of my head. My curls cascaded down in a free-falling waterfall, the ends bouncing with each movement I made.

Mary Elizabeth clapped her hands together excitedly. "Oh, Mae, it's perfect! You look so youthful, so radiant!"

Emmalynn and Sally Ann agreed, complimenting the playful style and how it showed off my high cheekbones. I, however, thought I looked more like I was heading to a cheerleading practice than my own wedding.

Just as I was about to voice my thoughts, the chime above the salon door tinkled, heralding a new arrival. All eyes swiveled toward the entrance, and a collective sigh echoed around the room as Hank stepped in. His tall, broad frame filled the doorway, and his handsome face broke into a grin when he spotted me.

"Ready for our counseling session?" he asked, his deep Southern voice making more than one heart flutter in the salon.

A chorus of *aww*s and approving murmurs filled the room. Helen gave me a final approving pat before ushering me toward Hank.

Mary Elizabeth piped up, her eyes twinkling with mischief. "Oh, Hank, isn't our Mae just the belle of the ball? Your wedding is going to be so gorgeous!"

Just as we were about to step out of the salon, Emmalynn asked, her voice a tad more serious, "Any leads on the missing teenager, Hank?"

Hank paused, his easy smile fading a touch. "Still working on it, Emmalynn," he said, patting her shoulder comfortingly. "We'll find her."

With that, we stepped out of the pink explosion of Cute-icles and onto the bustling sidewalk. Hank, the epitome of a Southern gentleman, gently took my hand and helped me climb into his truck. His touch was warm, sending a comforting shiver up my spine. Once we were both settled in, he started the engine, and we pulled away from the bustling salon, leaving behind a trail of feminine giggles and gushing adorations.

We maneuvered through the heart of downtown, moving past colorful boutiques and friendly cafés that had started to wind down after the day's trade. The town's charm lay in its nostalgic appeal and the familiar shops that populated its streets.

Hank was silent, his jaw set as he navigated the winding roads that led to Normal Baptist Church. His knuckles were white against the steering wheel. "I just wish they'd stop asking about the missing girl," he muttered, his gaze trained on the road ahead. "I'm doing everything I can."

Looking to change the subject, I asked, "Heard anything more about Etta's murder?"

His brow furrowed as he filled me in on the latest developments. "Blunt force trauma. There were tiny fragments of something found in the wound, but no weapon has been found."

His news spurred me into recounting the potential motives and suspects I'd been mulling over during my visit to Cute-icles. I described Edna, the woman from the Camping Cowgirls, detailing her interest in the brooch, her questionable presence at the yard sale, and her likely motive.

Hank listened, his eyes widening slightly as he took in the details. Then he frowned, acknowledging that he hadn't met Edna yet.

I didn't stop there, though. I went on to discuss Clay, how he and Etta had recently separated, and how it could tie into Etta's untimely demise.

Hank was quiet, listening attentively as he guided the truck along the dangerously curvy roads that bordered the dense forest and steep cliffs. The towering trees cast long, reaching shadows across the path as the sun began to set, bringing an end to a day that had been anything but ordinary. The golden hues of dusk painted the sky, setting a somber mood that matched our conversation.

As we approached the familiar white steeple of Normal Baptist Church, Hank took a deep breath, his fingers drumming against the steering wheel in thought.

"Why, Mae?" he asked, his eyes on the road but his tone serious. "Why do you want to stick your nose into Etta's death?"

I was taken aback by his question. Recently, he'd been fine with me looking into things. "What do you mean, why?" I wondered where this line of questioning was coming from.

"Well, it's just... It's dangerous, Mae. Murder investigations are no place for amateurs. And besides, why you? Why do you feel you need to get involved?"

I thought for a moment, gathering my thoughts. "Hank, I just... I just can't help it," I finally responded. "I care about the people in this town. I care about Etta. She was a part of our community, and she deserves justice."

"I understand, Mae," Hank replied softly, "but there's a line between caring and getting involved in a dangerous investigation. That's the job of law enforcement, and as a former cop, I can't help but worry about your safety."

"Hank, I'll be careful, I promise," I reassured him, reaching out and placing a comforting hand on his. "And it's not like I'm going to be out there chasing down suspects. I'm just... curious. I want to help in any way I can."

As he parked the truck in front of the church, he turned to me, his green eyes full of concern. "Mae, promise me you won't put yourself in any danger. I don't know what I'd do if anything happened to you."

His sincerity tugged at my heart. I knew he was thinking about the missing teenage girl—but I was no teenager.

"I promise, Hank," I said, squeezing his hand. "But if I stumble onto something that might help, I won't ignore it. That's the deal."

Hank sighed, running a hand through his hair. "I reckon that's the best I'm going to get, huh?"

I gave him a small grin. "I reckon so."

The Normal Baptist Church was no different than any other business in the area. It wasn't like Alex—um, Preacher Alex Elliott—provided marriage counseling out of the goodness of his heart. I mean, first thing when we walked in, he said, "I'm so glad to offer you this free service," as he passed the offering plate in front of us. "But if you feel you've gotten some valuable advice, you can show your appreciation."

And he let that dangle.

We were seated across from the preacher, his youthful face aglow with what I could only assume was the excitement of conducting a premarital counseling session. He was a good-hearted man, but there was a smugness in his eyes, as if his never-been-married self held all the answers to matrimonial bliss. I had to hold back a chuckle at the irony.

"What do you value about your relationship?" Preacher Alex asked, leaning forward with a genuine interest in his eyes.

Hank and I exchanged a glance, and a silent understanding passing between us. "Honesty," Hank finally said, his fingers twitching against his knee. "We're honest with each other."

"And the food," I added, grinning. "Hank values my cooking, and I value his ability to eat all of it without complaint."

The room filled with laughter, including Hank's deep chuckle, easing the tension. "Mae makes a mean pot roast," Hank added, causing a new ripple of laughter to wash over the room. It was our shared sense of humor that kept our bond strong, a fact that had me grinning from ear to ear.

The questions kept coming, some serious, some absurd. But we answered each one, sometimes in unison, sometimes with a teasing jab at each other.

Preacher Alex seemed pleased with our responses and continued with his inquiry. "Are you on the same page about children?"

At this, my heart rate picked up slightly. A flicker of unease crossed Hank's face. Hank and I had navigated this topic before, and it had led to a brief breakup. A raw nerve, you might say.

"It's... complicated," I admitted. "We want kids, sure, but... there are concerns."

Hank's eyes met mine in a silent understanding. "But it's something we've talked about a lot, and we feel we've resolved it as much as we can for now."

The counseling session moved on, with Preacher Alex delving into our financial plans, and Hank and I were once again in agreement. "We're planning on having joint finances," Hank said, his voice leaving no room for argument. "It's important for us to be transparent about where our money's going."

"But we're both savers," I added quickly, hoping to temper Hank's declaration with a bit of practicality.

Then came the question of where we would live. Living in the campground was a given, but the specifics were still up for debate. I was attached to my small, cozy camper, while Hank favored his larger, more luxurious fifth wheel.

"That's something we're still figuring out," I confessed, shooting Hank a sidelong glance. "I mean, my camper has everything we need, doesn't it?"

"Maybe for a gnome," Hank replied, grinning. "The fifth wheel has space, Mae. And a proper bed."

Our playful banter led to easy laughter, and in that moment, I realized that these differences, these debates, they were all part of the beautiful mess that was our impending marriage. And I wouldn't have it any other way.

"I'll see you two in a couple of days," Preacher Alex said, reminding us that we'd signed up for the speedy marriage counseling.

And of course, Hank threw a hundred dollar bill in the offering plate as Alex walked by us, holding it out.

As we exited the church hand in hand, I couldn't help but feel excited for our shared future, whatever it might hold.

CHAPTER EIGHT

The moon hung in the sky over the campground by the time Hank and I got back. We'd made a little detour after the premarital counseling to stop by the Dairy Bar for an ice cream. Hank had gotten the vanilla cone coated in hard chocolate, and I got the vanilla cone with extra sprinkles.

The Dairy Bar was a staple in the south. It was only a gritty little place that wasn't highfalutin' and served fried everything—I mean, fried okra, French fries, tater tots, pickles, chicken strips, and more. It didn't stop there—chicken sandwiches, cheeseburgers, sides of gravy, malts, ice cream. Any food you could think of that would clog your arteries.

The Dairy Bar was only open during the summer and was always packed. Hank and I had seen so many folks outside of our normal group of friends that we'd spent a little too much time visitin', which was why we got back to the campground so late.

As Hank and I strolled into the campground, the evening's quiet settled around us like a comforting shawl. The darkness was only broken by the sporadic glow of small campfires scattered throughout the grounds, casting an enchanting, flickering dance of light and shadow. Each fire had its own rhythm, its own story—families huddled together in soft murmurs, couples laughing in shared secrets, and lone travelers enjoying the quiet rustling of pages.

I wasn't sure if we were both trying to process our first session of pre-marriage counseling, as we'd not said a word in the truck on the way home. I kept my mouth shut and decided to let Hank talk if he needed to. His tension about our living arrangements once we were married hadn't gone unnoticed, and I could only imagine he was mulling over it.

Fifi and Chester were trotting at our sides, their noses pressed to the ground as they chased the scents of the day. They were as much a part of the campground as the towering trees and the crunching gravel beneath our feet.

The nighttime chorus of the forest was in full swing, the crickets playing their harmonious symphony. A pair of owls hooted back and forth across the forest, their calls echoing through the still air, and every now and then, the eerie cry of a distant coyote cut through the melody, adding a note of wildness to the tranquil scene.

Before us, the lake lay serene under the night sky, its still waters reflecting the twinkling stars and the silhouettes of the mountains looming in the distance. The moon's silver light traced a shimmering path across the lake, a celestial bridge in the still of the night.

With Hank's hand warm in mine, the scents of pine and the subtle smoky sweetness of the campfires filled my senses. The entire campground felt alive and magical under the night sky—a world apart from the rest of Normal, secluded in its own little bubble of wilderness and calm.

Every so often, a breeze would whip up from the lake, stirring the fires and sending sparks flying upward to join the stars. The air would fill with the soft whispers of the leaves, rustling against each other like the pages of an old book.

Every so often, I'd sneak a side glance at Hank as the moon caught his profile, and I could see him about to speak but stop himself. He definitely wanted to say something, so I remained silent, waiting.

Everything seemed more profound in the dark, every sound more pronounced, every smell more intense. This was our world, mine and Hank's. A place of peaceful nights, simple pleasures, and endless adventures. And I was ready to begin our shared life in this enchanted landscape.

As we rounded the lake past the bungalows, Hank gave my hand a squeeze. "This is just the beginning, Mae. Here's to a lifetime of stargazing and walks in the moonlight."

"Yes." I let go a sigh of relief when he didn't bring up the campers and start the debate of why his camper was better than mine. In the end, I knew it was virtually impossible for us to live in my tiny house on wheels, but I had to be able to bring myself to say it.

That might take some time. The little camper van and I had history. It was a connection that was unexplainable.

In the distance, the Camping Cowgirls began to set up their circle of chairs around the fire pit. I was reminded once again of how the campfire was a special kind of gathering place. There was something deeply human and connecting about the dancing flames, the warmth, and the smell of woodsmoke under the stars. It was like an open invitation to come, sit, and share stories. I've found that, often, people are more willing to bare their souls around a campfire than in the harsh light of day.

I loved that about this life—the camaraderie, the shared experiences, the opportunity to learn from the stories of others. That was the magic of the campfire. It wasn't just a way to keep warm or cook food. It was a gateway to understanding, to friendship, and to the kind of kinship that you find in unlikely places. It was a comfort and an invitation, beckoning you to gather round, pull up a chair, and become a part of the story.

And Hank and I did just that once we reached them.

"Do you mind if we join you?" I asked as Hank dragged over a few Adirondack chairs. "This is my fiancé, Hank Sharp."

The women lit up as much as the fire dancing in the middle of their circle.

"Hank, this is Charlotte, or Charlie, as she prefers to be called."

Charlie stood up, almost as tall as Hank, and Hank asked her about the group.

"I'm in my late fifties," she began, exuding an aura of confidence that was hard to miss as she told him about how she lost her husband to cancer. "Life is short. He always took me camping, but he did all the hookups and got the old girl all ready to take out, and I missed this life."

Her silver hair was cut into a short, stylish bob that framed her face and shook as she talked. "I was a travel writer in a past life, and I said to myself that I could still do it. I got me a job, and I took classes on how to drive an RV and pull a trailer." Her mischievous blue eyes squinted as the smile lines deepened.

I had no idea there were such classes.

"I got me a hitch and hooked myself up." Charlie was a natural-born storyteller, and her vivacious personality was the life of the Camping Cowgirl group. She pointed to the turquoise camper with pink flamingos painted on the side, a testament to her bold and vibrant personality.

"I write for *RV Traveling* magazine, and I met all these yahoos along the way." She snorted and motioned to the Camping Cowgirls who were still up and not tucked in for the night.

Then Edna, who I was most interested in, introduced herself to Hank. "I'm Edna Lee," she said. "I'm not as vibrant as Charlie."

Everyone around the campfire laughed and agreed.

"I'm a retired librarian, and I love the outdoors. I'm also a little bit older than Charlie." She went on to say she was in her mid-sixties. "I own the completely vintage Airstream Bubble." She peered over the rim of her glasses as she spoke, like she would if she were reading a mystery novel.

Or at least, that's how I pictured her.

"Edna prefers the quiet of nature and a good book over loud gatherings, but don't underestimate her. She's got keen intelligence and humor that often catches you by surprise," Charlie said.

"Which reminds me." Edna stood up before I could ask any questions about the day's events. By that, I meant Etta's murder. "Tomorrow,

I'm going to take you on a tour of my Airstream. But I'm going to bed now. It's been a long day of junking."

I wasn't about to push it. I knew Etta's murder wasn't going to be solved in a day, and there were plenty of other suspects to look at, including Etta's husband, Clay.

It seemed like an old cliché for the spouse to be the main suspect, but it wasn't. More often than not, the murderer was the spouse. In this case, there was motive.

Divorce.

There were all sorts of reasons to kill someone when you were in that position, but what could be Clay's reason?

Once Hank had gone back to his fifth wheel and I'd given Fifi her goodnight treat and belly rub, I found myself alone in the quiet of my little country farmhouse on wheels. The camper had a distinct homey charm that transformed it from a basic vehicle into a little slice of rustic heaven.

I flipped a switch and the twinkle lights came alive, casting a warm, inviting glow around the small interior. I loved my camper, loved the shiplap walls painted a crisp white, loved the gray wood floors that added a touch of chic to the camper's otherwise homey aesthetic.

The open-concept design meant my kitchen merged seamlessly with the small living area, all of it coming together to create a single functional space. My eyes fell on the quaint café table with its two chairs, both secondhand finds from the Tough Nickel, and the small leather couch that was just perfect for snuggling up with a book or, in my case, a sleuthing notebook.

In the bathroom, the tile shower and upgraded toilet were a vast improvement from what the camper originally had. And my bedroom, well, it was my little sanctuary, decked out with a comfortable mattress and a DIY pallet headboard, a four-drawer dresser that continued the distressed-look style, and, of course, more twinkle lights. The soft rugs on the floor added a touch of luxury, while the milk glass vases filled with fresh flowers brought a bit of the wild beauty of the Daniel Boone National Forest inside.

Closing the camper door behind me, I grabbed my trusty sleuthing notebook from a storage cabinet and plopped onto the couch. Opening the notebook, I started to go over what we'd gathered about Clay Hardgrove, Etta's husband.

Why would Clay kill Etta? I mused, running my fingers over the words we'd penned. The rumors about Clay planning to leave Etta, the whispers about fights over hoarding—all this painted a picture, but was it enough? As the twinkle lights cast shifting shadows around the camper, I promised myself that I would find out. The Laundry Club Ladies and I owed it to Etta and ourselves to uncover the truth.

As I flipped through the notebook, mulling over motives and clues, Fifi nestled against me, her little body radiating warmth. It had been a long day, and the night seemed to be just beginning. There was a mystery to solve, and I was intent on doing just that. One clue at a time.

"Fifi," I began, tracing a fingertip over the fluffy curve of her ear. She tilted her head at the sound of my voice, her dark eyes curious. "Today has been... It's been something. You know, when you're cooped up in here all day, you miss out on the town gossip."

Fifi's tail gave a soft thump against the leather of the couch, her head tilted inquiringly. I chuckled, reaching out to ruffle the fur at the top of her head.

"At Cute-icles, they were all talking about Clay Hardgrove," I went on, my eyes drifting over the notations we'd made about him. "They said he was leaving Etta... that they'd been fighting because of her hoarding."

Fifi gave a small yawn, her tiny pink tongue poking out between her teeth. She didn't understand the significance, of course, but her quiet company was comforting.

"Can you imagine that, Fifi?" I mused, continuing to pet her absentmindedly. "Could those fights have led to something... darker?"

Fifi's eyes slowly drooped, the soft, rhythmic motion of my hand on her fur lulling her to sleep. But even as I watched her doze off, my mind kept working, turning over the clues, the motives, the whispers from the town. And one question lingered at the forefront.

Was Clay Hardgrove capable of murder?

"If he is, Fifi," I murmured, more to myself than to the now-sleeping dog, "we're going to help make sure he pays for it. For Etta. Which means I'm going to have to call an emergency Laundry Club Ladies meeting for tomorrow morning."

CHAPTER NINE

The Laundry Club Laundromat was unlike any laundromat I'd ever seen. Even though I'd been able to get the washers and dryers up and running at Happy Trails Campground, I still did my laundry at the Laundry Club.

This was where my friends and I had gotten our beloved nickname. Maybe the way I felt the first day I'd walked into the Laundry Club had stayed with me, and that emotional nostalgia I continued to feel was what made me love this place so much.

"After you messaged us last night about our meeting, I took the liberty of checking out everything I could find on the internet about Clay Hardgrove." Abby tapped on her phone, her hair pulled up in a high ponytail, the way she wore it most days.

"Abby," I scoffed. "You didn't need to do that. I bet Bobby Ray was mad."

"Nope. He was snoring in the other room. So I found myself on the couch with a bowl of ice cream. I was going to fulfill some Tupperware orders but decided looking into Clay was much more exciting."

I stood at a tall table in front of one of the washing machines and flopped my fancy clothing bag, actually a pillowcase, over to dump out my dirty clothes. After I sorted the darks from the whites, I used the laundry detergent Betts offered her clients. It smelled good to me and did the job.

"You'll definitely want to hear what I found out." Abby sat cross-legged on one of the couches in front of the television section at the front of the laundromat.

Queenie was practicing some new Jazzercise moves and watching her reflection in the front windows. She said perfecting the moves was important, when I could imagine the class was probably huffing and puffing through the bouncing and grapevining and wouldn't pay too much attention to her. "I'm all ears." Queenie snorted. Her short blond hair was held back with a headband that matched her hot-pink body-suit, purple leg warmers, and bright white shoes.

"Firstly, Clay's reputation as a tough, demanding manager could indicate a propensity for anger and controlling behavior," Abby said while reading over an article she'd found about how Clay controlled every aspect of his business.

"That could have extended to his relationship with Etta, where her hoarding habits and potential defiance might have incited confrontations," Betts added to the conversation as she took the plastic wrap from a few boxes of new puzzles to replace old ones that were missing pieces. She moved things around before she stepped back from the puzzle station, looking pleased with her work, before she moved on to the book-club area in the far back.

"But was it enough for Clay to resort to violence?" I asked, playing the devil's advocate.

"That's not all." Abby continued to read. "Clay's past legal issues indicate that he was no stranger to high-stakes conflict. There's accusations of embezzlement—that suggests a possible desperation for money, a motive as old as crime itself."

"Oh, sugar." Dottie chortled from the coffee stand where she was doctoring up her cup. "You best believe it. A man can stand a lot of things, but if a woman starts spendin' all his hard-earned money on trinkets, well... that's enough to make a saint go rogue."

Then her tone shifted slightly, taking on a teasing note. "And don't even get me started on the hoarding. Lord knows, if a man can't find his favorite recliner under a pile of yard sale treasures or gets attacked by a mountain of plastic bags topplin' from a closet, he might just get a bit more than cranky. In fact, he might even get a bit... murdery." Dottie always added her own flair to the sleuthing and brought us back to reality with her snarky comments.

"Could he have had a financial motive for wanting Etta out of the picture? Perhaps her hoarding had drained their savings or their resources?" I asked, using Dottie's lively analogy.

"Maybe it's not that deep." Betts always brought us down to the basics. "Hoarding can create significant stress in relationships due to the physical clutter, financial strain, and emotional distress it can cause."

"How on this earth would you know anything 'bout hoarding?" Dottie asked, and it was a great question. "We all know you are a house cleaner, and you throw everything away. Even get paid by clients to organize stuff."

"I was a preacher's wife, and we did marriage counseling." Betts rarely talked about the daily activities she'd had to endure as a preacher's wife, and I'd never, ever thought about her sitting in on my counseling. "There's a lack of communication, and perhaps Clay felt unheard or ignored in the relationship. If Etta was consistently unwilling to address or work on her hoarding habits, it could have caused resentment and frustration for Clay." She shrugged.

"Go on." Abby leaned across the front of the couch and reached for the sleuthing notebook I'd brought with me this morning. Abby always took notes during our little snooping, um, sleuthing seshes.

"Financial disagreement is a big one. Etta's participation in the 127 Yard Sale might suggest a possible interest in selling and buying items. If she was buying a lot of items for her collection, this might have created financial strain or conflict. And that would lead to them being passionate for different things."

"Making them incompatible." Abby nodded. "People get married, and they do change and grow over time. It's possible that Clay and Etta simply grew apart."

"Or Clay grew apart." Queenie's headband slid down as she jabbed the air.

"Stress and anxiety caused by hoarding can also affect the mental health of the partner. If Clay found it emotionally draining or if it was affecting his own mental health, this could have been a significant reason for contemplating divorce," Betts said, surprising me by rattling off so many things that could've been a catalyst for Clay's motive.

Betts walked over to the coffee stand and began to clean out the stale coffee from the decaf pot to make more. "Like Abby mentioned, if Clay liked to be in control of things, he couldn't control Etta's hoarding. From what I remember of him and her, they did have parties but not with a house filled with trinkets. Clay might've been embarrassed by the state of their house, and they might have become an isolated couple."

"The only way to get answers to all of this-here speculation is to go visit with him." Dottie stood at the door of the laundromat with her cup of steaming coffee in one hand and an unlit cigarette in the other.

There was nothing more Dottie loved than to smoke a cigarette while drinking her coffee.

"Dottie is right," I said after Dottie pushed open the door to go outside. "What if we all make something to take to the house?"

"We already have the Bible Thumper meal train going." Betts, again, had all the answers.

"And you can drive the food to Etta's house?" I asked. "And that will get us in?"

Betts, Queenie, Abby, and I glanced around, side-eyeing each other as our little plan started to come together.

I joined Dottie outside the Laundry Club Laundromat.

"Welp?" Dottie snuffed the end of her cigarette out. "Now what?"

"Betts is going to finish my laundry while you and I go back to the campground." I put my hand deep inside my bag, pushing past the notebook to find my car keys at the bottom. "We are going to go get a tour of the Airstream Bubble."

With Clay's potential motives in mind, the idea that he could've killed his wife wasn't that far-fetched. It painted a disturbing image of what could have transpired between Clay and Etta. I was reminded once again of the severity of what we were dealing with—a murder, a life snuffed out too soon.

But Clay wasn't the only one on my list. Even though we knew her death was from a blunt force trauma to the head, we weren't really sure about all the details. Details that only an autopsy report would have. There was only one place I knew I could get a copy.

Granny Agnes, Hank's granny who works at the sheriff's department as the dispatcher.

But before I could go see her, I wanted to also collect my thoughts on Edna and her interest in the brooch and Etta. The only way to get in front of her was to take her up on a tour of the Bubble, and that was exactly what I was planning on doing.

CHAPTER TEN

P arked third in line down the campground, and probably the most striking of all, was Edna's unique 1955 Airstream Bubble, which had immediately caught my eye and probably that of anyone else coming and going from the campground.

"That's the most darlin' little camper." Dottie huffed and puffed as we made our way down the road to Edna's camper.

"It is, but remember, we are here to look for any clues about Etta's murder." I had to remind Dottie because she had a tendency to get wrapped up in conversation and not look around, which was what we were there for.

"Don't you reckon I know that?" she spat. The way she reacted, I feared she was about to have one of her hissy fits. "I considered Etta a friend. I want to know if Edna killed her."

"Just keep an eye out." I sucked in a deep breath to collect my thoughts before I walked up to the camper.

Looking at the outside of the Bubble was like stepping back in time, the sleek silver exterior hearkening back to an era when craftsmanship and individuality were celebrated. The body, made of aircraft-quality aluminum, was polished to a high shine and reflected the sunlight with a gentle gleam. The rounded shape from which it derived its name was as practical as it was charming.

It was tiny, but the camper didn't lack for personal touches. A string of pastel-colored fairy lights was strung under the awning, softly flickering in the sun and promising a magical ambiance come nightfall. Potted geraniums dotting the small outdoor area added pops of color against the silver exterior. A vintage folding lawn chair, similar to Dottie's find at Etta's curb alert, sat invitingly open under the awning, complete with a sun-faded cushion and a bright floral print that hinted at countless stories of camping adventures.

"Could you imagine packin' all of this stuff up when you leave a campground?" Dottie snorted and pointed to the potted plants. "Then havin' to haul it?"

"Yeah." I sighed, knowing all the particulars about weight distribution when it came to campers—dry weight and hauling weight.

When I stepped up to the door, I couldn't stop myself from taking a peek in the little front window dressed with delicate lace curtains.

"Looky at that cute little dinette." Dottie didn't just peek, she stuck her head up to the window and shaded her eyes so she could get a good look inside.

"Stop that," I told her and gave a hard knock on the door.

Edna popped her head out the door. "Hi," she said. "Come on in."

We stepped into Edna's renovated Airstream, marveling at the transformation she'd managed. It was like stepping into a cozy little cottage on wheels. The camper was done up in a charming retro style, with splashes of color and unique antiques adorning every nook and cranny.

Dottie was right. The polished wood of what appeared to be a petite dinette set, chairs upholstered in a cheerful yellow fabric, was darling.

Edna sat down in the dinette, cheerily explaining her love for antiques. She gestured at her pitcher of lemonade, and Dottie accepted while I passed.

The small table wasn't really big enough for three people, so I let Dottie keep Edna talking while I glanced around, touching a few things as if I were really interested in them, even though I was simply trying to find anything that would create a common interest between Edna and Etta.

"I spent so many years as a librarian, buried in books about history and antiques. Kinda gets under your skin, y'know?" Edna gestured at an intricately carved wooden trinket box. "Take this little gem here. It's a Victorian snuff box. Can't sell snuff these days, but the box is pretty, ain't it?"

Dottie, ever the gossip, kept asking questions a mile a minute about the unique pieces Edna had collected. Edna happily indulged her, providing the history of each one. Then Edna asked about the local post office.

"Just head down yonder," Dottie began, her Southern drawl deepening. "Once you pass the fork in the road next to that big ol' rock shaped like an arrow, just keep on straight for about three ball fields, maybe a smidgen more. Can't miss it."

As Edna furiously jotted down Dottie's instructions, I found myself drawn to a small display of antique jewelry. A pair of delicate gold earrings caught my eye.

"These are lovely," I commented, picking them up to get a better look.

Edna smiled, her eyes twinkling with pride. "I find pieces here and there during my travels," she said. "Nice way to make a little extra money. These earrings are from the early 1900s, believe it or not. I have a little online shop where I sell them."

"Where do you sell them?" I asked, wondering if I just might find something of Etta's there.

"Right there in that basket are a few of my business cards. Just take one." She pointed to the small counter. "My shop's URL is on there. Or it's got one of them fancy codes that you can hold your phone over." She tsked and turned back to Dottie. "The things they got nowadays just amazes me."

As Dottie continued to regale Edna with mindless conversation, I scrutinized the earrings, wondering if perhaps Edna had other, more personal pieces of jewelry in her collection. Pieces like Etta's missing brooch. It was a long shot, but it was a clue worth pursuing.

"How did you come across this little Airstream?" I asked.

"I acquired this gem from a kind old soul back in Arkansas." Edna folded her hands neatly on her floral tablecloth. Her delicate fingers traced the outlines of the small yellow daisies printed there. "Oh, the poor dear passed on, but his family didn't share his love for these vintage marvels. So I, having appreciated this beauty from a distance for the longest time, decided to swoop in and give it a new home."

Arkansas, I thought and made sure to remember it so I could google "Edna Lee" and "Arkansas" just to see what sort of information I might find.

Her chuckle filled the retro-inspired space, bouncing off the polished aluminum interior walls that shimmered against the reupholstered cushioned seats. "Surprisingly, many folks don't quite understand the worth of what they have. It's like your chair, Dottie."

Dottie, seated across from me on the refinished booth-style dinette, blinked in surprise. "My chair?" she echoed, her voice laced with confusion. "You mean that old green lawn chair I got from Etta's curb alert? That didn't cost me a red cent."

"That's the one," Edna confirmed, her gaze softening into something akin to nostalgic warmth. "Honey, do you have any idea what you've got your hands on?"

When Dottie shook her head, Edna leaned back against the repurposed cushions, launching into a remarkable account of the lawn chair's origins. It was allegedly from the 1950s, a limited-edition piece from a well-known manufacturer.

"I mean Etta told me the story about the original owner, Clara, but I didn't know all that history about the chair." Dottie's face light up. "I'm gonna take real good care of it now."

As Edna filled the cozy space of the Airstream with her antiques expertise, a fragmented memory fluttered in my mind. I recalled how Dottie and I had just gotten back from the curb alert, and the Camping Cowgirls were waiting for us.

When I was talking to Charlie, I remember Edna saying something to Dottie about the still-strapped-on-the-top-of-my-car dingy old lawn chair that I'd tried to talk Dottie out of taking from Etta's house that morning.

My mind began to wander. Could it be possible that Etta had thrown away something of real value? Something that, perhaps, Edna desired and could sell? Something she could kill for?

I plucked a business card from the basket.

"Say, Edna," I said, taking her from the conversation between her and Dottie. "When do you put items up for sale on your site after you purchase them?"

"Honey, if you want the earrings, I'm more than happy to sell them to you now, but I got those at one of the yard sales yesterday, and I am going to put them up on the site today." She got up from the table and opened a small drawer filled with different jewelry.

I couldn't help but notice her RV papers in the drawer too. That big zip packet that usually gets passed down from owner to owner.

"These items will sell so fast once they go up on my site." She shut the drawer and looked at Dottie as she took her seat again. "That's why I asked where the post office is located. It's good to get them out while I'm stopped."

While Edna was looking at Dottie, I laid my phone down on the counter.

"We better go," I said, abruptly ending the little visit. When Dottie opened her mouth to protest, I gave her a hard look that made her shut her mouth, pick up her glass of lemonade, and drain it.

"Yeah. We've got work to do before your dinner tonight." Dottie licked her lips. "That was some good lemonade."

"Thank you. I got them lemons off my own tree." Edna pointed to the window. "It's right out there."

"Your own tree?" I hadn't realized when we walked past all those potted plants that one of them was a lemon tree. "Can you show me?"

"Well now, y'all come on out here." Edna beckoned, rising from her booth seat with surprising agility for her age. The soles of her woven espadrilles tapped lightly against the laminate wood flooring, a rich hue that contrasted beautifully with the vintage Airstream's interior. "I want to show you my pride and joy."

With that, she ushered us outside onto a neatly manicured patch of green where a potted lemon tree stood among the other potted plants. The smell of zesty citrus lingered in the air, something I'd not noticed when we got here.

"Look at her," Edna murmured, her face lighting up with the affection of a proud parent. "Ain't she a beauty?"

A few bright yellow fruits hung from the tree, their vibrant color a stark contrast to the deep, glossy green of the leaves. Dottie and I shared a glance, both equally impressed by this tiny, thriving little garden Edna seemed to have put outside when we thought it all simply decoration.

"Now, the trick with these lovelies," Edna began, her fingers lightly tracing over the dark green leaves, "is that you've got to give 'em the right amount of sun and water. They're a bit like Goldilocks, if you will. Not too hot, not too cold. Just right."

She moved to a small red watering can near the base of the pot, its rustic charm fitting right into the picturesque scene. "They like their soil moist but not waterlogged. And let them have at least six to eight hours of sunlight a day." She demonstrated by carefully pouring water onto the base of the tree.

"Also, watch out for yellowing leaves. That means she's thirsty. And in winter, you need to protect her from frost, bless her heart." Edna gave a knowing smile, patting the trunk gently as if it were an old friend.

As I took in her words, my eyes wandered to the bright lemons hanging from the tree, and I couldn't help but let my thoughts drift back to Etta.

"Do you mind if I take a photo of the tree?" I asked, patting around my shorts for my phone.

"Of course I don't." Edna's voice held pride.

"Darn." I shook my head. "I think I left my phone inside. Can I run in and get it?"

She nodded and Dottie started to carry on with her about the other little plants while I went back inside.

Smart girl, I congratulated myself and grabbed my phone from where I'd left it on purpose, then I quickly opened the drawer where the stashed jewelry and RV packet were kept.

With one eye on the small window to the outside, I unzipped the packet and searched for any document that would have the name of the person Edna had purchased it from. There was no way this Airstream didn't come without some sort of document telling its history—it was truly an antique gem that would still cost almost into the six figures today.

"*Voila,*" I gasped, my eyes open wide, when I came across a bill of sale from Lou Dimond to Edna Lee. I tapped the front of my phone to bring up the camera and took a photo of it.

I made a mental note to dig deeper into this man's sudden death that Edna had mentioned. Something about it just didn't sit right. Sure, people passed away unexpectedly all the time, but in the context of Etta's murder, every detail seemed magnified.

How did you die, Mr. Dimond?

Returning my phone to my pocket, I moved to the small porthole window, peering out at Edna and Dottie. The sun cast a warm, golden hue over the campground, painting Edna's frail silhouette with a gentle glow as she laughed at something Dottie said. Despite the chuckles and easy conversation, a flicker of unease sparked in my gut.

Edna, with her antiques knowledge, folksy charm, and friendly demeanor, could easily be seen as a harmless elderly lady. But what if this likable personality was nothing but a cover? People had been known to hide behind the most unsuspecting of facades. I watched as she gestured animatedly to the lemon tree, her face lighting up with passionate delight.

Could this seemingly innocent woman be capable of murder? I chewed on my bottom lip, contemplating the thought. It felt almost ludicrous to even consider it, but I'd learned in my amateur sleuthing adventures that sometimes the most dangerous villains were the least likely ones.

"Got it!" I hollered on my way back out to where they were, shutting the small door behind me. "Dottie, you ready to go?"

"Yep." Dottie rocked back on the heels of her shoes then tossed a lemon in the air and caught it. "Thanks for the lemon."

"You're welcome. Now be sure to come back for the potluck and place setting contest tonight." Enda strolled along with us to the edge of her camper pad. "I'll have fresh lemonade. Not that what you had inside wasn't fresh, but it's a day old, and tonight's is going to be so tasty."

"Will do," Dottie called. Both of us waved goodbye to Edna.

"We will if she's not sitting in the cell at the sheriff's department," I muttered, so quietly even Dottie didn't hear me.

Or she didn't bother trying to hear me as she lit up a cigarette.

CHAPTER ELEVEN

As we ambled away from Edna's shiny silver Bubble Airstream, Dottie and I made our usual rounds of Happy Trails to check on our guests. The campground buzzed with life, campers everywhere indulging in the tranquil respite of the wilderness.

Children splashed about in the lake, their delighted laughter echoing across the water, while others paddled around in swan-shaped boats, their faces flushed with excitement. The rich scent of campfires wafted through the air, merging with the sweet aroma of roasting marshmallows and grilling hot dogs. Groups of campers lounged around the unlit firepits, sharing stories and laughs, enjoying the gorgeous day. Some were heading off into the woods, their backpacks heavy with supplies, while others were toting kayaks, eager to explore the lake's serene expanse.

We walked past the little bungalows offered by the campground, each a charming cabin nestled amidst the trees. Their spacious back decks overlooked the vast expanse of the forest, a tranquil view that took my breath away every time. These were always gobbled up first by families who wanted to hold reunions, bachelorette and bachelor parties, and other large gatherings. The bungalows were just about as popular as the campers we had available for rent, and our waiting list was at least six months out.

"What on earth is going on in that noggin of yours?" Dottie asked when we walked by the tent sites where a few brave souls were setting up camp within the deeper woods.

"You know," I began, leading the way up the campground toward my camper van, "I can't help but wonder if Edna killed that guy in Arkansas just to get her hands on that Airstream."

Dottie turned to me, her eyebrows raised in surprise. I showed her the picture of the bill of sale I'd found tucked away inside Edna's Airstream naming Lou Dimond the former owner.

"Well, I'll be!" Dottie laughed, shaking her head in amusement at my sleuthing antics. "You left your phone inside on purpose, didn't you?" The smoke danced out of her nostrils as she stopped just shy of my camper to snuff out what little was left of her cigarette before she put the butt in her pocket.

I walked up and opened the door of my little home so Fifi could dart out. She took off toward Dottie, letting Dottie give her one good rub before the dog headed toward all the guests that she could find outside. During the day, Fifi was allowed to roam as she wanted. There wasn't any danger from critters trying to snack on her, as they wouldn't show themselves with the sun shining brightly and the people kept them away.

"I guess we will have to keep her on the suspect list, though I was hoping you'd changed your mind." Dottie shook her head.

By the time we circled back to Dottie's camper, Fifi was running free, her little legs kicking up dust as she dashed around joyously. The sight brought a smile to my face. Dottie and I both watched Fifi for a few moments, chuckling at her antics.

My gaze then fell on the lawn chair from Etta's last curb alert. I snapped a few photos and scrutinized it closely, hoping to identify any markings that might reveal more about its origins.

"I can't help but get a chill when I recall you and Bea talking about the lawn chair when I was with Charlie doing their arrival paperwork."

CHAPTER TWELVE

"Loooouuuu." Dottie's long Southern drawl nipped at my eardrum as she stood behind me, my phone in her hand, as she read off the name on the bill of sale of Edna's Bubble Airstream. "L-O." She began spelling it.

I stopped typing the name into the search engine and looked over my shoulder.

"What?" she asked with a snarl. "You know how people are. They can spell a name so many different ways. It could be L-U. And don't you want to git it right the first time?" There was a bit of a snark to her tone.

"L-O-U," I repeated, turning around and pecking at the keys.

"Dimond. D-I-M…" She stopped. "See, here. You'd think 'Dimond' would be spelled like the gem. But it ain't."

She curved the phone around my head and showed me, even though I recalled the way it was spelled from when I took the photo. "Now, type in 'obituary' and this town. Okay, hit that return button," she instructed me after I'd typed in his full name, like I didn't know how to work a computer. "Sorry."

She must've felt me tense. "No, I'm just wondering… When I hit the button, what is going to happen?"

I hit Return, and many results popped up, but it was one obituary from the same Arkansas town a couple of years ago that got my attention. The link took me to the funeral home where I could read the entire obit as well as note the date of death.

"What is the date on the bill of sale?" I asked.

"May." Dottie gasped and squealed, "Date of his death was May!"

"It doesn't mean anything," I reminded Dottie. "It just means that when she told us she'd gotten it when he died, it was the truth."

"Does it say how he died?" Her brows perked. She moved her finger in front of the screen, gesturing me to scroll up so she could continue to read. "Right there." She jabbed the screen. "It says right there he died suddenly. Sud-den-leeeee." She rocked back and forth, crossing her arms across her body, then started her pacing behind me.

"Dottie, you have to stop walking." It was distracting me from trying to copy and paste some of Lou Dimond's family members' names into different search windows so I could at least see if there was someone we could contact.

It was truly unbelievable what you could find out about someone on the internet. The fact that I could just put in this man's name and where he lived and pay two dollars to get all the information I needed from the white pages to not only contact his wife but also all of his children.

"Best two dollars ever spent," Dottie said in a hushed whisper. She reached across me and snatched up her pleather cigarette case that held her entire pack of cigarettes in the snap section and her lighter in the front expandable pocket.

"I'm gonna need me a smoke." She sucked in a deep breath and headed straight for the door, getting out of my hair for a few minutes.

Restless energy zipped through my veins like the fireflies that would be lighting up Happy Trails Campground that night as I perched before the computer. Lou Dimond's obituary was pulled up on the screen, his face both gentle and foreign as he smiled from a time now past. His wrinkles appeared carved deep with age and laughter, and a thin veil of gray hair decorated his head like frosted spiderwebs.

I held my phone, already dialed with his son's number. My hand hovered over the call button, a sheen of cold sweat coating my palm as I psyched myself up for the conversation. It wasn't every day that someone got a call asking them if they thought their father's sudden death was actually murder because someone wanted his antique RV.

The phone rang in my ear, an eerie echo of unanswered anticipation, as I recited my mental script, my voice a soothing lullaby against my pounding heart. *Hi, this is Mae West from the Happy Trails Campground. I'm wondering if we could chat about Edna...*

The line was picked up, and a brisk, no-nonsense voice declared, "Yeah, what do you want?"

Startled, I stumbled over my words, "Um, h-hi, I was just wondering about—"

"Not buying it, lady." The man cut me off, his voice an avalanche, burying my sentence under a mountain of impatience.

"But... I just wanted to..."

"Nope, not interested!" he barked over my protests, the verbal equivalent of a door slammed in my face.

"Now then..." A sigh escaped me, feeling a little more comfortable about calling one of these numbers without Dottie hovering over me.

At that precise moment, the door of the office creaked open and in breezed Dottie with Fifi at her feet, Dottie's eyes going round as saucers as she caught sight of my flustered face and the phone clutched in my hand.

"I... just want to talk to you about..." I fumbled and shook my head at her.

With a quick stride and a twinkle in her eye, she plucked the phone from my fingers, and with a gusto that belied her Southern charm, she quipped, "Now, you listen here, sonny. You're chattering faster than a squirrel on a caffeine high. I suggest you zip those lips and give my friend Mae here a chance to speak, or you'll be answering to me. And let me tell you, sugar, my bark's got a bite! This is about your father's murder!"

The soft hum of the air conditioning mingled with the distant chattering of the campground radio, filling the small office with a familiar, comforting white noise. The musty scent of old paper and the sharp tang of fresh ink permeated the room, mingling with the earthy aroma of the campgrounds wafting in through the slightly open window. I took a deep breath as Dottie handed the phone back to me, her eyes twinkling with her Southern mischief.

"Okay," I breathed into the phone, holding it a little tighter in my hand, my voice shaky despite my resolve. The cold plastic against my ear felt alien, a sharp contrast to the warm chatter I'd come to associate with our office. "Dottie, my colleague here, mentioned something about your father's... murder?"

There was a beat of silence, a breath held in anticipation as the man on the other end stuttered out, "Mur... mur...?"

Dottie, never one to shy away from a bit of theatrics, piped up from across the room, her melodious voice ringing out clear and strong. "Murder, sugar. That's right. Now, are you gonna chat with our girl Mae, or do I need to do the talking?"

I jerked my finger up to my lips to get her to stop talking. She took the moment to walk over to her desk and open the jar of dog treats so she could give five of them to Fifi.

There was a sigh of resignation from the other end, a gusty exhale that echoed my own anxiety. "Okay, okay. I'm all ears."

I looked at Dottie and shrugged. Her antics had worked out in her favor this time. I took a moment to gather my thoughts, Dottie's supportive nod serving as the catalyst for my next question. "Your father's Airstream... Did he ever mention a woman named Edna Lee?"

The man's laughter was sharp, brittle—harsh punctuation in our serious conversation. "Edna? Yeah, my dad used to talk about her. He said she was like a dog with a bone about that Airstream. Just would not let go."

My curiosity piqued, I pushed further. "Can you elaborate?"

"Well," he began, his voice taking on a nostalgic tone that belied his earlier laughter, "she was relentless. Showed up at the oddest times. Interrupted our family dinners, tried to outbid everyone at charity auctions. Heck, she even tried to persuade Dad to sell at my sister's wedding. Dad always just shook his head and told her it wasn't for sale. He loved that thing."

"But after he... passed, did Edna..." I hesitated, unsure how to phrase my question.

The man cut in, his voice a soothing balm to my spiraling thoughts. "Bought it almost immediately. Look, my dad died of a heart attack. We were on a family vacation when it happened. We didn't put it in the obit, but that's what happened. I don't know what you're trying to find, but I promise, it's not murder."

His words hung in the air, a sudden veil of silence falling over the office as I processed his revelation. "Thank you so much for your time," I said.

He interrupted. "Wait, is she in trouble? Is something wrong with the Airstream?"

"No, no. Nothing like that." I couldn't get off the phone fast enough now. "Thank you so much for your time, and I'm sorry about your dad."

I hit the off button.

"What was that?" Dottie snorted.

"What?" I asked and gnawed the inside of my cheek, staring at Lou's photo.

"Sorry about your dad? He's been dead for years." Dottie's eyes moved past my shoulder and stared out the window behind me that looked over the campground.

"It was the polite thing to do, Dottie. Mary Elizabeth would be proud." My shoulders raised to my ears and fell as the breath escaped me.

"Speaking of Mary Elizabeth." Dottie pointed to the window, and I turned around. "She must think you're home today."

"I am supposed to be home today. It's your day at the office." I clicked off the browser window and stood up. "It looks like Edna is not a killer and the next person we need to look at is Etta's husband. We need to follow up on his threats of divorcing her because she's a hoarder."

My phone's ringtone sang out with the chorus of "Happy Trails."

"You good here?" I asked Dottie before I took Mary Elizabeth's phone call.

"Go on. If I need ya, I'll call." She pointed to Fifi, who was already taking a nap, exhausted from running around the campground while Dottie and I were fiddling with our dead-end lead on one Edna Lee. "I'll take care of her."

"Are you sure?" I asked before I looked down at the phone to hit the green button before the call went to voicemail.

Mary Elizabeth was talking before I could say hello. "Where are you? We have the cake tasting at Cookie Crumble."

"I'm up at the office." My gaze took in Dottie's open mouth. Disappointment in how I'd forgotten about the small detail of the wedding cake was written all over her face.

Even Dottie knew this was bad. And if Dottie knew, then it was awful.

"I'll be right up there to get you" was all I heard before Mary Elizabeth hung up on me.

I turned back to Dottie. "If you're sure you don't mind keeping an eye on her"—I nodded at Fifi—"I'll be sure to bring you something back."

"That goes without sayin'." She snorted. "I'll see what else I can dig up on Clay while you're gone."

"That would be fantastic." I heard a car drive up before the horn honked. "That's my ride."

Apparently I wasn't quick enough gathering my things. The crisp chime of the office's doorbell cut through the comfortable quiet as Mary Elizabeth waltzed in. The bell's shrill ring was about as subtle as my mama's entrance, which was always something to behold. Her vibrant sundress swished around her legs, the floral pattern a burst of summer against the office's familiar, worn interior. Her bright eyes swept the room before landing on me, a mix of disbelief and exasperation washing over her features.

"Oh, Mae," she sighed, her Southern drawl rich and warm despite her clear distress. "We've talked about this. You can't meet Christine Watson wearing those..."

I looked down at my jeans and T-shirt then back up at my mama. "I'm comfortable."

She shook her head, her long hair bouncing with the movement, and placed her hand on the strand of pearls around her neck. "Comfort ain't the point, darlin'. We're going to taste wedding cakes at Cookie Crumble. It's an occasion, and you're gonna dress accordingly."

Before I could protest, she'd turned on her heel and was striding toward the door, leaving me with no choice but to follow.

I didn't bother turning around to see Dottie snickering. I could hear it.

The humid air hit me as soon as I stepped out of the office, the familiar scent of the campground filling my lungs before we got in her car. Mary Elizabeth talked all the way down the campground. She yammered on about the wedding: the location, the catering, the guest list, the contract for the reception at the Old Train Station event barn that I hadn't yet signed. I was halfway to drowning in a sea of wedding details by the time we pulled up to my camper.

"Do you even care about your wedding?" Mary Elizabeth finally asked, her eyes wide with concern. I could see the genuine worry etched into her features, making me feel a pang of guilt.

I sighed, turning to face her. "I care about marrying Hank. That's the only thing that matters to me. I'd marry him with a bread tie as a wedding band if I had to."

The look of horror that swept over her face was almost comical.

"Mae!" she cried, clutching at her chest. "A bread tie? Are you tryin' to give me a heart attack?"

Laughing at her dramatics, I squeezed her hand reassuringly. "I'm just saying, I don't need all the fancy stuff. I just need Hank."

She took a deep breath, shaking her head at me. "Well, you might not need it, but you sure as sugar deserve it. Now, go on and change. We've got cakes to taste."

Minutes later, we rolled smoothly through the heart of downtown's winding roads in Mary Elizabeth's car. The quaint town, with its whimsically charming shops nestled in restored cottage homes, was bathed in the soft gold glow of the afternoon sun. Deters Feed-N-Seed hardware store cozied up next to Trails Coffee, not too far from the Normal Diner. Just down and opposite Deters was the Tough Nickel. There were a few more shops other than the Smelly Dog Pet Groomers and the Laundry Club Laundromat, like a chic boutique and a new bookshop I'd yet to explore since they opened.

As we headed out of town, I looked out the window at the cliffs and gorges standing resolute, their shadowy figures mirrored in the tranquil lake's glassy surface down below. Nature had painted an exquisite canvas of deep greens and rugged browns offset by the vivid blues of the clear sky. Cotton-wool clouds lazily meandered above us, their shapes shifting in the gentle breeze. It would've been a perfect afternoon to lay in the hammock at Happy Trails Campground, catching a snooze or two.

Who was I kidding? If I was at Happy Trails, I'd be trying to find out all I could about Etta's life and the days before her death.

"Got a group booked for the whole of fall, Mae," she was saying, the corners of her eyes crinkling with delight. "Your old friends from Perrysburg. They're all excited about the wedding."

"Mm-hmm," I responded absentmindedly, my gaze tracing the scaffolding surrounding the building of the new Cookie Crumble. The sign in the window flashed Open, and customers were inside.

Mary Elizabeth parked the car. "And we should make it a Hawaiian-themed party. You'd look great in a hula skirt, Mae." A cheeky grin played on her lips as she glanced my way.

"Yeah, sure, Mary Elizabeth..." My response trailed off as her words filtered through my preoccupied mind. I shook my head, a wry smile playing on my lips. "Wait, what?"

Mary Elizabeth's laughter filled the car, a delightful, lighthearted sound that took me back to my childhood. "Caught you daydreamin', sugar," she teased, her eyes twinkling. "You've got your mind on something else. It wouldn't be a certain murder mystery, would it?"

I sighed, confessing, "I've been digging into Etta's case, Mary Elizabeth."

Her cheeriness faltered, her lips pursing in concern. "Oh, Mae! That's dangerous territory. Let Hank and his boys handle it." She wagged her finger at me. But then, as quickly as her worry appeared, it vanished. A curious gleam lit her eyes. "But speaking of Hank, any news about that poor missing girl?"

I couldn't help but laugh. That was Mary Elizabeth—admonishing me one moment and indulging in the same curiosity the next. I guess she wouldn't be Mary Elizabeth if she wasn't a charming bundle of contradictions.

"Let's get in here and eat some sugar," I said, vowing to myself that I would be as present as possible.

Stepping into the newly refurbished Cookie Crumble was like being enveloped in a sugary, warm hug. The aroma of fresh coffee, vanilla, and butter seeped into our senses, the hint of cinnamon and chocolate teasing our appetite.

The light from the honey-gold pendant fixtures hung low over the polished counter, illuminating the cozy interior and highlighting the striking contrast between the pristine white beadboard wainscoting and the warm wood tones of the reclaimed flooring.

Mary Elizabeth and I were greeted by Christine Watson, her apron vibrant violet against her white baker's uniform. Her welcoming smile was as sweet as the confections she masterfully crafted. "Mae, Mary Elizabeth, it's so good to see y'all," she called out, her Southern lilt inviting and warm.

"Christine, dear, this place is as stunning as one of your layer cakes," Mary Elizabeth said, her gaze sweeping across the cozy bakery.

Christine chuckled, leading us to a beautifully decorated table laden with an impressive spread of treats. Pumpkin-spiced mini cupcakes sat next to petite lemon tarts and vanilla cream puffs, each delicacy more enticing than the last.

"These, darlings, are some of the goodies I've prepared for your wedding." Christine pointed out each platter. "The pumpkin-spiced mini cupcakes offer that quintessential autumn feel, the tart lemon is a delightful palate cleanser, and the light, fluffy cream puffs conclude the feast on a sweet note."

Mary Elizabeth squealed in delight, clapping her hands together. "Oh, Christine, these sound absolutely delightful! Mae, isn't this exciting?"

I nodded, my eyes drawn to a small table off to the side. "And the cake?" I asked, unable to take my eyes off the three-tiered masterpiece decorated with cascading marzipan leaves in shades of russet, gold, and burgundy.

"Oh, that," Christine said, beaming proudly, "is a replica of your wedding cake. I wanted to capture the essence of autumn and your love story—beautiful, simple, and sweet."

I was rendered speechless. The cake was indeed as Christine had described. It felt as if she'd poured our love into every detail, making it a perfect representation of us.

"And then," Christine continued, her eyes twinkling with delight as she moved to the side of the table, revealing another creation, "I have your groom's cake. Customized, just for Hank."

A stunning confection stood on the adjacent table. The two-tiered cake was crafted to tell the tale of Hank's adventurous life. The base layer was iced to resemble a topographic map, skillfully piped in a spectrum of greens, browns, and blues to denote mountains, plains, and bodies of water. The detail was impeccable; you could trace Hank's journey from his days as a sheriff in the lowlands, moving into more treacherous territory in his role with the FBI, and finally to his life as a ranger.

On the top tier, a fondant figurine stood proudly, binoculars hanging from his neck. Next to him, a miniature fondant camper rested against a backdrop of mountains, with tiny trees scattered around to complete the scenic portrayal. It looked exactly like Happy Trails Campground.

The icing on the cake, quite literally, was the silver star that rested atop the whole creation, a nod to his former role as sheriff. It was a masterpiece that spoke volumes about Hank's dedication to his job and his love for the great outdoors.

"Christine, it's perfect!" I exclaimed, admiring the detail that had gone into crafting the cake.

Her thoughtful representation of Hank in fondant and frosting was more than I could have imagined. Even Mary Elizabeth was silent, her eyes wide as she took in the sight of the remarkable cake.

Christine beamed at us, clearly proud of her creation. "Your love story is unique, and I wanted to ensure that every aspect of it is celebrated, even in cake form. This is Hank's journey and his passion, and I couldn't help but let it inspire me." She gave me a huge hug.

"You have outdone yourself." There was a tear in my eye. The realization set in that in a few months, I was going to be Mrs. Hank Sharp.

"Let's dig in." Christine handed Mary Elizabeth and me a fork. "Go on. Try them all."

Mary Elizabeth and I spent the next thirty minutes devouring the delectable treats, making a few jokes about how we weren't going to fit into our fancy wedding dresses if we didn't stop.

"It's a tasting," I reminded them. "Not a full-on eating of all the cookies, cupcakes, tarts, and cakes."

"They are so yummy." Mary Elizabeth smacked her lips together. "My goodness. Too bad Hank couldn't come. You know he's investigating that teenage girl's disappearance for her parents."

Christine looked at me all bright-eyed. "I heard about her. That's awful. That and Etta Hardgrove's death. Poor Keely." Christine tsked.

"Keely?" I asked.

"Etta's daughter. She and her friend Adrienne are working here for the summer while home from college." Christine picked up the plate of treats after Mary Elizabeth and I had forced ourselves to walk away from the table.

I glanced around and noticed the afternoon sun streaming in through the floor-to-ceiling windows, bathing the charming bakery in a soft, golden glow.

The new Cookie Crumble was more than a bakery; it was a haven of love, sweetness, and warmth. I sucked in a deep breath to clear my cloudy, sugary mind and think what questions I could ask Christine about Keely and if Keely had mentioned her mom and dad's relationship.

As I was ruminating over the cake, my mind swirled with questions about Etta. I needed to find a way to ask Christine, but I was interrupted by a shift in conversation.

"Where's Keely today, Christine?" Mary Elizabeth inquired, her gaze flicking to the empty counter. "Isn't she working over the summer?"

"Actually, she's taken the day off, Mary Elizabeth," Christine replied, a touch of concern etching lines onto her otherwise youthful face. "She is going to take some personal time for obvious reasons."

I took a deep breath, gathering my courage before asking, "Did Keely mention anything about... well, her parents, Christine?"

Christine's eyebrows shot up, clearly taken aback by my question. "Well, no, not particularly," she admitted. "But Adrienne might know more. They are roommates, after all."

She gestured to a young woman behind the counter, her auburn hair tied back into a messy bun and flour dusting her apron. "Adrienne, could you come here for a moment?"

Adrienne looked up, her sea-green eyes curious. Wiping her hands on her apron, she walked over to join us. "What's up, boss?"

"Adrienne, this is Mae. She's a good friend of mine." Christine introduced me with a smile. "Mae, this is Adrienne. She's Keely's roommate at the college."

Adrienne extended a flour-dusted hand, grinning broadly. "Nice to meet you, Mae. Is this wedding-cake tasting for you?"

"It is," I said, nodding. "I was hoping you could help me with something."

Here goes nothing, I thought to myself with a smile.

"Adrienne, Keely's quite lucky to have you as a roommate. You two must share a lot with each other?" I asked, watching her for any signs of discomfort.

Adrienne nodded, a fond smile curling on her lips. "Yeah, we do. Keely's like the sister I never had."

"I understand Keely's been dealing with a lot at home," I continued, cautious, noting how Adrienne's expression shifted subtly, a mixture of concern and surprise playing across her features.

Adrienne's smile faded, her gaze drifting over to the door as if she expected Keely to walk through it any minute. "Yeah... her mom... Etta, right? She has a problem with hoarding. It's been tough for Keely. Once Keely had wanted to bring a few college friends home who wanted to go hiking. They ended up in a huge fight because Keely asked her mom to clean the house and her mom refused."

I gave a sympathetic nod, my mind whirring with questions. The timing was right to delve deeper. "Adrienne, this might be a sensitive subject, but has Keely ever mentioned anything about her parents... possibly getting a divorce?"

Adrienne seemed to freeze, her eyes widening in surprise. "Divorce," she echoed, seemingly taken aback. "No, Keely never mentioned anything like that. But I have to be honest and say I did overhear Keely crying and talking to Andy, her boyfriend. She didn't tell me, but I heard her say her parents might get divorced. She was pretty upset and I knew she'd've told me in time."

"I'm not sure if they were getting divorced," I confessed, keeping my tone calm. "That's what I'm trying to figure out. I want to help Keely in any way I can."

Adrienne seemed to mull it over, her brows furrowed in thought. Finally, she nodded, meeting my gaze with a determined expression. "I'll talk to Keely, see if she's okay. And if she mentions anything... I'll let you know, Mae."

With that, Adrienne turned on her heel and went back to the counter, leaving me with more questions than answers and a palpable tension that seemed to hang heavy in the air.

The soft chime of the door echoed in the room as I stepped into the Laundry Club, immediately spotting Betts and Abby huddled together. As I approached, I noticed the table in front of them was practically overflowing with food. Casseroles of various types, homemade bread and pies, and, as the centerpiece, Ethel Biddle's banana pudding. The sweet smell of the delicacies mingled with the scent of detergent and freshly laundered clothes.

Betts spotted me first, her expression brightening. "Mae, look at all this food we've got for the Hardgroves!" She waved her hand proudly over the collection of Southern comfort food.

"Wow, that's quite a spread," I agreed then dove into the reason I was there. "But listen. I talked to Adrienne, Keely's college roommate, and she told me a few things we need to consider."

Betts and Abby exchanged curious looks before turning their attention to me. Abby put her hand out, gesturing for the notebook we used to track our investigations, her pen poised and ready.

"So," I began, my gaze shifting between my friends, "Adrienne mentioned a couple of incidents. One was about Keely being upset because Etta wouldn't clean the house so she could bring her college friends home. They got into a major fight about it."

Abby's pen was already scratching furiously against the paper, recording every word. I watched as Betts's eyebrows furrowed, her concern evident.

"There's more," I continued. "Keely is the one who suggested to her father that he divorce Etta. Adrienne accidentally walked into this conversation between Keely and Andy. She said Keely was crying and Andy was consoling her."

The room was silent for a few moments as they digested the information. Abby was still writing, her brows knitted together in deep thought.

Betts was the first to break the silence. "Mae, that's some heavy stuff. Do you really think Keely could be involved in her mother's death?"

"It's a possibility we can't ignore," I conceded. "We have to consider all the options."

Abby finally stopped writing, setting the pen down and sighing deeply. "This is... big. But Mae's right. We have to consider it."

The gravity of the situation was apparent in their faces, the jovial mood from earlier replaced by a solemn determination. Yet the need for answers, the desire for justice for Etta Hardgrove, outweighed our trepidation.

"All right then," Betts finally said, gathering up some of the dishes. "Let's head over to the Hardgroves'. We deliver comfort food and hopefully get some answers."

Nodding in agreement, we prepared to depart, the tantalizing scent of home-cooked meals a comforting constant amid our growing unease.

If there was one thing I knew about us Southern folks, it was our knack for disguising our intentions. Who would ever suspect a group of women delivering food as sly detectives? Perhaps, between mouthfuls of Ethel's banana pudding, we could finally crack this case wide open.

The soothing hum of Betts's van was almost drowned out by our anxious chatter as we made our way toward Etta's neighborhood. Betts's hands were tight on the wheel, her eyes flicking between the winding road and us in the rearview mirror.

Abby was sitting in the back of the van with all the cleaning supplies, not caring one bit as she flipped through the sleuthing notebook, while I stared out the window, watching the familiar landscape of our small town pass by.

"Okay." Betts finally broke the silence. "We have to be smart about this. We can't just start asking questions outright. We need to be subtle."

Abby nodded, her pen hovering over a blank page in the notebook. "Yeah, we can't spook them. It'll look suspicious."

I turned my attention away from the kids playing in the park we were passing, their high-pitched laughter fading in the distance.

"Agreed," I said. "We have to act normal, as if we're just there to offer our condolences and nothing more."

"We should probably divide the questioning between us," Betts suggested, her Southern accent always more pronounced when she was stressed.

"That's a good plan," Abby agreed, jotting it down. "We should also keep our eyes open for anything that could be a clue."

"Absolutely," I said.

Our plans were interrupted by the sight that greeted us as we rounded the corner onto Etta's street. The 127 Yard Sale was in full swing at her house.

Bargain hunters and curious neighbors were picking through items displayed on tables and blankets spread on the lawn. A part of me was in shock. *How could they carry on with this in the wake of such a tragedy?* I wondered.

"Oh my goodness," Betts breathed, slowing the van. All of our faces were pressed up against the windows. "I can't believe they're still doing this."

"I guess life goes on, even after..." Abby's voice trailed off, her gaze fixed on the scene outside.

"All right," I finally said, pulling myself together. "Let's stick to the plan. We're here to deliver food and find answers. Let's do just that."

Betts slowed the van down and stopped into the first spot available. She shoved the shifter into park but kept the van running with the air conditioner on high. She turned to her right so she was facing me and looking back at Abby.

"Okay," Betts said. "We need a solid plan before we walk through that door."

"You're right." Abby flicked a loose strand of hair out of her face and bit her lower lip. She clasped her hands together and rested them on the notebook. "First things first. We act like we're just dropping off meals. Nothing more. The meals are our cover."

"Agreed." I glanced back at the dishes from all the people in town. "We offer condolences, make polite conversation. But remember, we're there to listen more than we talk."

"Absolutely," Betts said. "We've got to watch and listen. We might hear something useful. Abby, you've known Clay the longest. You handle him. Ask about his feelings, how he's coping... and tread lightly."

"Got it." Abby nodded, her pen making swift motions over the page. "And Mae, you should talk to Keely. Keep the conversation light, about college maybe, and then gently try to bring up her mother."

"Will do," I agreed, my mind already buzzing with good questions to ask. I wanted to know more about Keely's relationship with her mom and how she felt when her mom didn't want to clean up the house so she could bring her friends from college home.

"Good," Betts said with a nod. "I'll handle the others. Friends, neighbors... I'll make small talk, see if they say something that catches my ear."

"And we should also keep our eyes open for anything unusual around the house. Anything out of the ordinary that we could take note of," I added, leaning forward, a determined look on my face.

"Let's be extra observant while we're inside. But remember, we have to be subtle. We can't let them catch us snooping around," Abby cautioned, looking between Betts and me.

"We'll be careful," I assured her, my heart pounding with a mixture of anxiety and anticipation.

"Let's do this," Betts finally declared, her hand gripping the van's steering wheel tighter. It was a side of her I loved! "And let's hope we find the answers we're looking for."

As we stepped out of the van, each of us carrying a couple of dishes, we steeled ourselves for the task ahead.

The cheerful bustle of the yard sale was a stark contrast to the somber mission we were on. It was a surreal experience, walking toward a house of mourning that was, at the same time, the center of the town's activity.

As we made our way toward the house, we moved through the throng of the yard sale. Etta's front yard was littered with tables laden with an assortment of goods, ranging from well-worn books to mismatched sets of china and tarnished silverware to knickknacks that had no doubt seen better days. The eclectic mix of items was as chaotic as it was poignant, remnants of a life now reduced to a roadside sale.

Among the tables was a young woman. She was standing behind a table that displayed a collection of beautiful brooches. Each one was intricate and unique, like tiny pieces of wearable art. The sunlight sparkled off the jewels embedded in them, casting rainbow specks across the faded wooden table.

They reminded me of the ones Etta had taken to the Tough Nickel. She must've had an expansive collection.

The girl's fair hair was pulled up into a high ponytail, and she wore a faded jean jacket adorned with a variety of patches, a testament to her vibrant, youthful spirit. Her bright blue eyes were animated as she fiercely negotiated with an elderly bargain hunter over the price of one of the brooches.

"These brooches belonged to my mama," she was saying, her voice tight with emotion, her hands protectively cupping a particular piece— a silver sunburst studded with diamonds. "She loved these more than anything. They're true antiques. And someone already took her favorite... I won't let these others go for any less than a hundred dollars."

The bargain hunter walked away, and with a sigh, I meandered over to the girl. "Hello there. I couldn't help overhearing your conversation. My name's Mae, and I was a friend of your mama's."

Her eyes shone with tears instantly, her voice catching as she said, "Really? You knew my mama? She was just the best, wasn't she?"

"Yes, she was," I said, gently patting her hand. "And she sure had a good eye for beautiful things, just like this brooch you're holding."

She nodded. The tears welled up and spilled over.

"Anyways, I'm with the Normal Baptist Church Bible Thum—er, Bible group, and we have a lot of food. We know you and your daddy will need to eat, and during trying times we know it's hard to remember to feed ourselves." I noticed her eyeing both casseroles I was holding. "All the food is either in foil dishes or paper so they can be recycled or thrown out." I couldn't imagine what on earth it would be like if Betts had to return all of them.

"We have more in the van. If you'd like to take these, I'll go get the rest." Betts handed her two dishes to the young girl.

"That way, you can show me to the kitchen where we can find room for these in the fridge." I was grateful for Betts's quick-on-her-feet thinking.

"Of course, follow me," she replied, leading the way toward the house. As we started moving, noise from the yard sale tables faded behind us.

"I'm Keely, by the way," she said.

"Yes. I realized it was you when I came up to the table." My heart hurt for her. "I'm truly sorry for your loss, Keely. I... I know what it's like to lose your mother. I lost mine in a house fire when I was a teenager, along with my entire family."

I swallowed the lump in my throat that always seemed to materialize whenever I brought up my past. I left out how I ended up with Mary Elizabeth, who fostered and then adopted me. It wouldn't matter to Keely at her age.

"Thank you, Mae. I'm... I'm still trying to process everything," Keely admitted, her voice barely a whisper.

She headed across the lawn more quickly, balancing the dishes Betts had given her, and I followed behind. Not that I was a trained detective, but I'd paid enough attention to Hank as well as nosed through enough crimes to always keep an eye open for anything.

Keely seemed innocent enough, which made me wonder if she were a true suspect, but I wasn't ready to take her off the list yet.

Following Keely through the hallways of Etta's home was like tiptoeing through a time-worn museum where the artifacts of someone's life lay jumbled in haphazard towers of memory. Each room was a crypt of curiosities, an archaeological site that spoke volumes about a woman's existence held within the confines of this ordinary home. Old newspapers formed papery barricades, their headlines frozen in time, each page yellowed by the passage of years. Vintage clothes lay draped over chairs, each stitch a story of past style trends, and furniture pieces from decades past stood like silent sentries.

A rainbow of knickknacks crowded the shelves, an array of ceramic animals, mismatched china, and dusty picture frames with long-faded photographs. Cabinets strained under the weight of seemingly endless collections of DVDs and VHS tapes, each labeled in Etta's neat script, a nostalgic relic of another era. Amidst the sea of accumulation were islands of housewares—tarnished silverware, chipped mugs, rusted cast-iron skillets—each an echo of a meal served, a guest welcomed, a family nurtured.

"I'm so sorry for the mess," Keely apologized, her voice a light tremor in the gloom of the cluttered rooms, her cheeks blooming with a blush of embarrassment. She nudged a precarious tower of cardboard boxes to make way, the dim hallway light glinting off her fair hair. "Mama... She liked to collect things, hang on to memories, maybe. We tried persuading her to clear it out, but she was stubborn."

Her laugh was dry, edged with frustration and sorrow. "I almost wish we could open all this to the yard sale. It'd make things a lot easier," she murmured, casting a disheartened glance over the tsunami of her mother's life.

I let her talk and tried not to show how overwhelmed I was feeling just being in here for a brief time. I couldn't imagine how she felt. There was no way this was something Etta had done over the last few years. Her hoarding must've been a lifelong disease Keely'd had to deal with as she grew up.

This was a serious motive, enough to keep Keely on my list of suspects.

Despite the overpowering chaos of things, there was a peculiar homeliness seeping from the walls of the house. It was filled with Etta, in her love for things and stories, her stubborn refusal to let go of the past. Keely, walking amid the wreckage of her mother's obsessive collecting, seemed like a lone sailor lost in a storm of dusty relics and faded memories.

"Was your mom a hoarder?" I asked.

There was a momentary pause in her step as though I'd caught her by surprise. "You seem like a smart woman. You tell me," she said, looking over her shoulder before we walked into the kitchen.

The kitchen, however, was an oasis of calm within the cluttered storm. What must have been the old heart of the home, it echoed Etta's love for cooking and baking. The room was a step back in time with mustard-yellow appliances, faded linoleum flooring, and walls adorned with once-vibrant floral wallpaper now dulled with age. Here, at least, order reigned. The countertops were relatively clear, the stove clean, and an aged oak table stood humbly in the middle of the room. It was a tiny alcove of normalcy in the bewildering maelstrom of the house, a testament to a woman's love for the simple pleasure of feeding her family.

"We didn't mind all of that in there, but Daddy put his foot down when it came to the kitchen." Keely laughed as if she were recalling how that conversation went down between her parents. "A little teapot here. A little plant there." She pointed to the open space between the ceiling and the top of the cabinet. "Mom thought she could sneak in things without Dad noticing, but he had taken photos of the kitchen, and every day when he came home, he'd pull out those photos and compare them to what was in reality."

She walked over to the refrigerator and opened it. As she continued her recounting of things, she moved around the condiments and a few other half-filled plastic containers.

My eyes wandered to the bowl of spaghetti topped with sauce and a few meatballs. Was that Etta's last meal? There was only one bowl, and after hearing what Sally said Adrienne had told her about the separation, my heart sank.

I imagined Etta sitting alone at the table with a full bowl of spaghetti. Alone. It reminded me of Hank, which reminded me of Adrienne.

"I'm getting married this fall." I handed Keely one of the dishes I was holding after she'd made room in the refrigerator for the food Betts had given her. "I went to the..." I was just about to delve deeper into the conversation with Keely, when out of nowhere, a familiar voice called out.

"Hey, Keely! How much is this one?" Adrienne, who I'd met at the Cookie Crumble earlier, came into the kitchen, holding up an ornate candlestick that caught the afternoon light in a play of warm glows. Her green eyes widened in surprise as she recognized me. "Oh, it's... Mae, right?" she stammered, seemingly taken aback. A trace of discomfort passed over her face, and I could tell she was uncertain how to handle this unexpected encounter.

"Yes, it's me, Adrienne," I said, grinning. "I was just about to tell Keely here about the amazing spread Christine put on for me earlier today at the Cookie Crumble. I really appreciate all the help you gave us with choosing the menu for the wedding. Your suggestions were spot-on."

Adrienne blinked in surprise before a small, relieved smile crossed her face. She had clearly expected a different line of questioning from me, but now she seemed to ease into the situation quickly. "Well, it was no trouble at all, Mae. Christine knows her stuff, and I'm just glad I could be of help. I hope your wedding turns out to be everything you've dreamed of." Adrienne wagged the candlestick in front of Keely, beckoning for an answer.

"Look at this." Keely peeled the edge of tin foil off the banana pudding and curled it back. "Banana pudding."

"I want a bowl," Adrienne said, apparently forgetting all about the asking price of the candlestick.

Keely put the pudding in the middle of the table with a few bowls and spoons.

As I settled into a worn, cushioned chair at the kitchen table, I said, "I can't resist a taste of Ethel's famous banana pudding." I gave them a sheepish grin.

Keely smiled in return, her eyes lighting up with a spark of life despite her sadness. "You know Mom always loved pudding. Said Ethel's was the best in the whole county."

Adrienne nodded, pulling up a chair next to Keely, her eyes scanning the collection of homemade dishes that now crowded the kitchen counter. As she scooped a spoonful of pudding onto a plate, she glanced in my direction, her gaze hesitant.

"You know, Mae," she began, her voice just above a whisper, "when I met you earlier at the Cookie Crumble, I didn't know you knew Keely since you were asking about her family... about Etta and Clay."

The room fell silent.

Keely's spoon froze halfway to her mouth, her eyes darting between me and Adrienne. It was then that Betts and Abby made their entrance, carrying the last of the food from the van. Their laughter and chatter filled the silence, but the tension remained, a thick blanket settling over us.

"Ah, here's the last of it," Betts announced, setting down a pie with a flourish.

Abby followed suit, but her gaze was keen, taking in the stillness that had settled over the room. "What's going on?" she asked, glancing at me.

Before I could answer, Keely turned to me, her eyes searching. "Mae, what exactly were you asking Adrienne about earlier?"

CHAPTER THIRTEEN

Keely's brows drew together, her eyes darkening with a cloud of anger sweeping over her. Her knuckles whitened around the spoon she was still clutching, her jaw set.

"Why exactly are you poking around in my family business, Mae? We're dealing with enough without strangers prying into our lives!" Her voice rose.

Before I could respond, the front door creaked open, the sound echoing through the cluttered house. Footsteps approached, and I heard a voice I assumed to be Clay Hardgrove as he called out for his daughter. "Keely? You all right?"

A moment later, a younger man's voice chimed in—presumably Keely's boyfriend.

"Keely?" Clay's voice came from the hallway, his tall figure soon filling the kitchen doorway. His eyes flicked from his daughter to me, confusion clouding his weathered face. The younger man lingered behind him.

"Get them out, Daddy." Keely's voice trembled, her eyes shimmering with unshed tears. "Mae's been asking about you and Mom, about... about our family."

Clay's gaze hardened, focusing on me. "Is this true?"

"I... I can explain," I stammered, feeling their accusatory gazes.

"No! No more explanations!" Keely exploded, slamming her spoon onto the table. The clang echoed through the silence that followed, and the spoon skittered across the table, splattering banana pudding everywhere.

"You don't belong here, Mae! You aren't police. You aren't even a friend of the family. You're just a... a busybody poking around where you don't belong. I want you out!" Keely screamed, tears rolling down her face.

I reeled back from her anger, a wave of guilt washing over me. I wasn't here to upset Keely or Clay, but they deserved the truth, deserved to know what I was doing.

"Keely," I began, my voice softer this time, "I'm sorry. I didn't mean to upset you or invade your privacy. I just... I thought I could help. I thought maybe... your mom's death wasn't just a coincidence."

But as the words tumbled out, I saw Keely's face close off, saw the anger in her eyes replace any shred of understanding she might have had.

"And now you're saying my mom's murder wasn't just a... a random act? That's it! Get out! Get out now!"

"Keely..." I tried again, but the look in her eyes stopped me. There was a raw hurt there, a deep pain that I had unwittingly stirred. I realized then that my good intentions had only added to her suffering.

Clay's stern gaze stayed fixed on me, the unspoken command clear in his eyes.

With a heavy sigh, I nodded, rising to my feet. "I'm sorry, Keely."

As Betts, Abby, and I walked toward the door, I could feel the heavy weight of Keely's eyes on my back, a reminder of the pain and turmoil she was facing. And a reminder that good intentions weren't always enough.

As we wound our way through the labyrinth of stacked magazines, dusty furniture, and assorted trinkets, the anger in Keely's voice still ringing in my ears, the noise of the bustling yard sale outside provided a sharp contrast. The bright sun streaming through the windows did little to lighten the weighty atmosphere of the house.

Just as we neared the front door, a voice came out from behind us. "Wait," Clay said, his voice softer now, filled with a grief that made my heart ache.

Betts, Abby, and I stopped, turning back to face him. When I looked at Clay's face, the crinkles around his eyes were deeper, like they had been etched in by the weight of sorrow.

He took a deep breath, as though bracing himself for a task he'd rather avoid. "I know who you are, Mae." His hands fidgeted with the edge of his flannel shirt. His eyes darted between Abby, Betts, and me. "I know your fiancé Hank from years of being in the law enforcement areas of the park. He left to do his own thing, right?"

"He did." I gave him a haphazard smile, trying not to say too much.

He nodded then moved his gaze to Betts, and he managed a small, sad smile. "And Betts, I know you from the church. You and Etta always did have a laugh together."

The familiarity of his words, the small remembrance of Etta's laughter, did a little to melt the tension. Yet, the sorrow was still there, hanging around us like a shroud.

"Look." Clay swallowed, his voice hoarse. "Etta and I, we... We were on the outs. But I still loved her. And I can't shake the feeling that something terrible happened to her, something more than a crazed yard sale-goer."

There was a desperation in his voice, a pleading look in his eyes. It was the look of a man who had lost his partner and was floundering, desperate for answers. "I don't think Al Hemmer is... He's not doing enough." His fingers clenched into fists, the knuckles pale. "Do you think... Could you ask Hank if he'd look into it?"

I was taken aback. Clay Hardgrove, asking for our help? It wasn't what I had expected, but the plea tugged at my heartstrings. "Clay," I said, choosing my words carefully, "Hank's not taking on any cases right now." I wasn't going to tell him Hank was consumed with the teenage runaway case. "But Betts, Abby, and I... we're trying to get to the bottom of this. We could help, if you'd talk to Keely about it."

Clay looked stunned, then, slowly, he nodded. It was clear he was willing to do anything, even entrust his estranged wife's case to a group of amateur sleuths, for a chance at finding out the truth about what happened to Etta.

"Mae is right." Abby pointed to me and then Betts. "We have a way of talking to people and getting them to open up. Just like we knew you and Etta were divorcing because of her issue with hoarding."

Clay's eyes widened at Abby's statement. His gaze bounced between us, surprise mingled with a hint of admiration. He sighed, running a hand through his hair and nodding slowly.

"You're right, time is of the essence." He nodded, his eyes weary. "Wait here. I'll talk to Keely."

As Clay disappeared back into the maze of clutter, the three of us shared a glance.

Abby was the first to break the silence. "Do you think we should ask him if he has an alibi?" she asked, her voice dropping to a whisper. Betts and I looked at each other, contemplating Abby's suggestion. "I mean, we've not stuck with the plan at all."

But Clay had been through enough, and frankly, it didn't feel right to corner him at that moment. "If I've learned anything while trying to look into murders," I said, trying to put it better than saying we were meddling as Keely had accused, "I've learned that plans change."

"I think we should see if Keely will talk to us. Then we kinda draw it out of her with good questions." Betts had a great suggestion.

Clay returned before we could reach a decision. All three of us buttoned up our lips and stood straight when we heard Clay finding his way back through the clutter to us.

His face was pale, but there was a determined set to his jaw. "Keely will answer your questions," he said, meeting each of our gazes in turn. "She's still in the kitchen."

The three of us shared a glance. Silently, we all agreed not to question Clay about his alibi, not right then. We navigated our way back through the obstacle course, and when we entered the kitchen, the tension was palpable.

Keely, Adrienne, and the tall, lanky young man I assumed to be Keely's boyfriend stood huddled around the table, remnants of the banana pudding smeared across the surface.

Keely was dabbing at her eyes, the strain clear on her face, while Adrienne stayed close by. There was an air of hostility between Adrienne and the young man. His arms were crossed over his chest, and his posture was rigid, avoiding eye contact with Adrienne. Adrienne, on the other hand, seemed too focused on Keely to pay him much mind, but I could see a hint of discomfort around her eyes. I couldn't put my finger on it, but the tension had to be due to the strained relationships, unspoken words, and simmering emotions, all stewing in the wake of Etta's death as the people who loved her sat silent.

Then Keely looked at the two of them, saying, "I don't know what I'd do if it weren't for you two."

Adrienne put her hand on Keely's right shoulder, and the boyfriend put his hand on Keely's left.

"Mae, I'm sorry. I guess I owe you an apology," Keely said, looking my way.

"No. There's no apology needed." My jaw and eyes softened. I saw a little bit of myself in her. "I told you I understand because I lost my family. There's going to be days of confusion, frustration, and sadness that will cover you like a dark cloud, but with the support you have here, you're going to get through this."

"Mae is right. Her family was murdered." Abby's words shocked all four of them. "Oh, I thought you said you told her."

"I did, but I didn't tell her all the details." Still, I didn't care who knew, so I gave them a brief history before I said, "I didn't think the local law was doing enough to solve the years-old murders of my family, either, so I began to dig until I uncovered who did it and why they set my family home on fire when I was spared."

"And that's how we all got really good at this," Betts noted, only it wasn't with the death of my family that we'd all come together to actually solve some crimes.

It all started the day I'd walked into the Laundry Club Laundromat under the cloud of suspicion that I'd killed my ex-husband. It just kinda spread like wildfire that the nosy Laundry Club ladies were pretty darn good at putting together a murder puzzle, and it sure did help that we were pretty good at gossiping.

After all, there was some truth and information involved in telling tales. Sometimes we had to pluck out the smallest of details to find the killer.

Etta Hardgrove's murder was no different.

I knew it was best for me to sit next to Keely, let her know I was on her side. *For now.* I took the seat next to her and put my hand on her arm. She pulled away.

"Keely, Clay," I began, my fingers smoothing over the aged oak tabletop, "we'd like to ask you about Etta's hoarding habits. Her collections. Did she ever mention any pieces of particular importance or value?"

Keely's gaze dropped to her hands folded in her lap. She took a deep breath before she replied, her voice barely more than a whisper, "Mama... She always had a lot of stuff. Some folks thought it was junk, but she loved it all. Said each piece had a story."

Clay shifted in his seat, leaning his elbows on the table, his brow furrowed. "Etta never really singled anything out, though. She didn't let many people see her full collection, especially not in the house. She was secretive... protective of it."

Betts chimed in then, her gentle voice carrying a serious undertone. "Did she ever tell you about anyone who was particularly interested in her collection? Someone who might've thought something valuable was hidden among her things?"

A moment of silence hung over us as Keely chewed on her lower lip, her eyes darting over to Clay.

"There was... There was one man," she said hesitantly, glancing back at her father, who was watching her with intense eyes. "Orville Jenson.

He's a dealer in antiques and curiosities. Always wanted to get a look at what Mom had in here."

"And did she ever let him?" Abby's question was quiet, but it made Keely flinch slightly.

"No," Clay answered gruffly, shaking his head. "Etta didn't trust him. He was too eager, too pushy. Wanted to buy everything off her, but Etta wasn't selling. Not to him."

"Anything in particular?" I asked.

"Not that I know of. I tried not to get into all of the way her brain worked with all this…" He stopped as if he couldn't bring himself to say it, then finally added, "Stuff."

"That's what Mom said about Dad's perception of her collections." Keely gulped. She reached in the middle of the table to pick up her napkin so she could dab her eyes. "He looked at it as stuff."

"It is stuff." Clay frowned. "I guess it was not to her."

Keely's boyfriend walked over with another napkin and handed it to Clay.

"Thanks, Andy." Finally, Clay had said the young man's name. I was glad I didn't have to ask because it just felt a smidge awkward.

Abby's pen scratched against her notepad, diligently recording each bit of information. "And after Etta refused to sell to him, did Jenson's behavior change? Did he become more aggressive, perhaps?" she asked.

Keely nodded, casting a troubled glance at her father. "He did. He wouldn't stop calling, showing up at the house unannounced. Even started sending her threatening letters. Mom was scared, but she wouldn't back down. She said those pieces weren't his to have."

My heart jumped at this revelation. This Orville Jenson seemed to be a man obsessed, potentially dangerous. He had a motive and, apparently, didn't shy away from threatening behavior. He definitely warranted a closer look.

"Well, thank you both for being honest," I said, meeting Clay's and then Keely's eyes. "We might not have much to go on yet, but every bit of information helps. We will do our best to find out what happened to Etta. You have my word."

Abby and I started to leave, and I turned to see what Betts was doing.

"I just can't." Betts shook her head. "You told me just a few minutes ago how Etta thought a lot of me. If I've learned anything through my own hardships the last couple of years, it's to not let something go past if you can't shake it from your thoughts."

Betts turned and looked at me and Abby. She sucked in a deep breath as though she were trying to gain courage to tell us something.

"What's wrong?" Abby asked her.

"I know we weren't going to ask them for their alibis, but I can't just stand here and pretend we don't think these two had something to do with Etta's murder."

The room held its breath after Betts's statement. Clay's hand, which had been resting on the kitchen counter, stiffened. Adrienne gasped, her fingers clutching the dish towel she had been holding. Andy's eyebrows knitted together, his lips pressing into a thin line. Keely's reaction was the most dramatic; her eyes widened, and she visibly recoiled, as if Betts's words were a physical blow.

After no one said a word, Betts began again. "You know," she said, her voice steady even though her hands twisted together, betraying her nervousness. "Etta... She meant a lot to us. She was a pillar of this community, and we want to make sure her death isn't in vain."

Everyone's gaze was drawn to Betts, their shock giving way to comprehension. Betts didn't back down; instead, she held their gaze, her chin jutted out in determination.

"We..." Betts glanced at Abby and me, her eyes flitting nervously between us. "We need to ask where you all were when Etta... when it happened," she finished, compassion in her voice.

Keely's face tightened, her eyebrows furrowing. It looked as though she was about to argue, but Clay placed a calming hand on her shoulder, causing her to stop.

"You're right," Clay agreed, his voice barely above a whisper. "We're just as eager for answers." He turned toward a side table, rummaging through a pile of papers. He produced a receipt and handed it to me, his hands slightly trembling. "Keely and I... we were in Slade," he said. "We went to look at an apartment there. We made a deposit. Here's the date and time."

As I took the receipt from Clay, I noticed his fingers were slightly cold. The date and time stamped on the receipt coincided with the estimated time of Etta's death. It seemed like they had a solid alibi.

"I already provided this to Al Hemmer," Clay added. His eyes were red-rimmed and glossed over with unshed tears. "We're not hiding anything. We just want to find out who did this to Etta."

The silence that followed was broken by Andy, who had been silent for most of the conversation. "I was at college. You can ask my roommate," he offered, shrugging nonchalantly. "And Adrienne, she was at the Cookie Crumble all day. There's a timecard and cameras."

Not that we had asked for Adrienne or Andy's whereabouts, but it was endearing how the two saw themselves as family.

"Do you mind if we get a look at the shed out back?" I asked.

"Sure. If you can get in there and not hurt yourself." Clay shrugged. "I'll take you."

Even though Clay had provided a pretty solid alibi and had already told Al, I couldn't help but feel the buzz of the tension in the air as we stepped out of the house, the bright Kentucky sun creating a stark contrast to the somber mood that hung over us. Adrienne and Andy excused themselves to go back to the yard sale where there were plenty of buyers looking over Etta's goods. Images of Etta and how she'd have been telling everyone the history of the item they were interested in quickly faded.

Clay, Abby, Betts, and I crossed the yard. I could feel the curious gazes of the yard sale attendees boring into our backs. Keely stood in the doorway behind us, her expression hard and distrusting.

Though I wanted to look at the spot where Etta's body had been found, I averted my gaze. It felt disrespectful, as if I were intruding on her final moments of peace. Instead, my attention was drawn to Clay, who led us toward the back of the house, his shoulders tense.

The backyard was a canvas of overgrown weeds and neglected

greenery. A tangled mess of bushes replaced what I could tell was once a manicured lawn, and the house's shadow loomed ominously over it. The animated chatter from the yard sale grew distant as we trekked toward the rear of the property, replaced by the gentle rustle of wind through the trees and the distant chirp of a sparrow.

In the corner, hidden by the onslaught of flora, was the shed, which looked as though it had been untouched for years. Its wooden panels were worn and grey, the paint peeling back to reveal a battle with time and elements. The sagging roof groaned under its burden of leaves and branches, and the rusty hinges on the door squeaked under the slightest breeze.

The scene gave off a peculiar odor, a blend of damp soil and decaying timber, mixed with an underlying hint of mold. It was a scent that clung to the back of your throat, a persistent reminder of the dilapidation before us.

Clay stopped a few paces from the unstable structure, his hands tucked deep into his pockets as he stared at it, his expression grave.

"Haven't been in there in years," he confessed, his voice low. "It's all Etta's hoard. I just... couldn't bring myself to deal with it. She recently told me she'd been digging through it and apparently had done a couple of curb alerts."

My ears perked up, but I kept my eyes on the old shed, believing Etta had probably pulled that old lawn chair out of there, dragging it across the back yard before she left it on the curb. I smiled as I recalled the story Etta had told about it. *A story for every piece.*

I watched Abby's and Betts's reactions. Abby's brows furrowed as she studied the structure, while Betts merely crossed her arms over her chest, her gaze darting around the yard as if trying to piece together the events leading up to Etta's death.

The sight of the shed, forgotten and filled with unspoken history, ignited a feeling of unease within me. Its worn-down appearance felt ominous, like a silent witness to a tragedy we were only beginning to uncover.

Abby and Betts mirrored my sentiment. Abby shifted uncomfortably next to me, her usually cheerful face serious. Betts, usually so stoic, showed a flicker of concern in her gaze as she scanned the area. Despite the disquiet, an unspoken agreement hung between us. This shed, decrepit as it may seem, held potential answers. It was a relic of Etta's life, a cryptic jigsaw piece in the puzzle of her death, and we were intent on figuring it out.

Drawing in a deep breath, I reached for the door of the shed. A large, misshapen rock served as a makeshift doorstop, its rough texture scraping against my fingers as I nudged it aside. It resisted at first, stubbornly rooted in its position before it grudgingly yielded, leaving a furrow in the dirt as it rolled away.

The door creaked gloomily as I pulled it open, revealing the darkness within. A strong scent of age, damp, and mold wafted out, making us all crinkle our noses in distaste. Silence enveloped us for a moment as we stood there, staring into the shed's gloom, our anticipation palpable.

Taking my phone out of my pocket, I activated the flashlight function and cautiously pointed it into the shed's interior. Shadows scattered, fleeing from the light that intruded on their domain. Dust particles floated aimlessly in the beam from my phone, performing a ghostly ballet.

As the light spread, we got a glimpse of the chaos within. A surreal landscape of neglected lawn ornaments lay haphazardly, some whole but many more in various states of disrepair. Twisted shapes of concrete animals, their features eroded by time and neglect, lay among fragments of what once might have been gnomes or fairies. They were like specters of a garden past, their glory days long gone.

The silence around us deepened as we absorbed the scene. There was a sense of intruding on a sacred space, of being privy to a part of Etta's life that was meant to be hidden.

As I moved the light around, a sudden gleam caught our attention. I froze, my heart hammering in my chest as I slowly redirected the light back to the source. A splotch of something dark and glistening was smeared on one of the concrete statues. A cold dread spread through me as realization dawned.

Blood.

My phone slipped from my hand, plunging us back into darkness. The echo of its impact against the ground seemed deafening in the shocked silence that followed.

As I stood there, frozen in shock, my mind raced. What did this mean? Was it connected to Etta's murder? A chilling thought formed: *did we just stumble upon the scene of the crime?*

The others seemed equally stunned, their faces pale. Clay's eyes were wide, his mouth hanging open in disbelief. Abby held a hand to her mouth, her eyes wide. Betts, always the stoic one, stared at the darkness, her face unreadable.

"I think we just found the murder weapon," I said and slowly bent down to pick up my phone to call Sheriff Al Hemmer.

CHAPTER FOURTEEN

The thought of us finding what seriously looked to be the murder weapon didn't sit too well with Al Hemmer.

In fact, he didn't even take our statements once he got to the Hardgroves' home. He told us all to go home and he'd call upon us if he needed us.

But that didn't stop me, Betts, Abby, Dottie, and Queenie from talking all about it once we gathered at Happy Trails Campground for the Camping Cowgirls shindig. They were having a potluck on the covered patio of the recreation building where they were also hosting a place setting contest. Blue Ethel and the Adolescent Farm Boys plucked away on their instruments nearby, tuning up for the after-supper concert when Queenie would be teaching some of her line dancing moves.

As the sun began its descent, casting a warm orange glow across Happy Trails Campground, our little group huddled inside the office, each of us with a steely determination lighting our eyes. Abby was dutifully reading from her notebook, her glasses perched on the end of her nose, while Betts, Queenie, and Dottie listened attentively.

"Well, this is a pickle if I ever saw one," Dottie exclaimed, her Southern accent wrapping around her words like honey. She tapped an unlit cigarette on top of her desk, packing the end. "You're telling me we've gone and found the murder weapon before Sheriff Hemmer did? That man wouldn't know his elbow from his rear end."

"We can't be certain it's the murder weapon, Dottie," Abby cautioned, her voice the epitome of reason. "But it seems likely, given what we saw at the Hardgroves'."

Betts chimed in, her brow furrowed in concern, "It has to be. We saw it." She shivered.

Before we could delve any deeper, the office door opened. "When I didn't see y'all outside, I thought you were in here." Agnes Swift shuffled in, waving a file in the air, her grey curls neatly coiffed and a wry smile playing on her lips. Agnes was a force to be reckoned with, and having her on our side was an advantage.

"I brought Edna back," she announced, waving a hand toward the doorway signaling outside. "Al didn't have anything to keep her on. She called her boy, and he got a lawyer on the phone."

"Heavens," Queenie said, her voice shaky. "Did Al tell you about what Mae and them found in the shed in Etta's backyard?"

"Did I?" Agnes discreetly slid the file across my desk.

"How are you?" I walked over to her, ignoring the file for the moment to give her a hug.

"The question is, how did the marriage counseling go?" She looked at me. "You're still gonna be my granddaughter, right? I need someone who's going to take care of me when I'm old."

"Even if I weren't going to be your granddaughter, I'd still take care of you," I told her. She was already getting up there in age, though she was still very spry.

"Oh no," Abby cried out. "I'm so sorry we didn't ask you about the counseling session."

All of the ladies gathered around to hear what I had to report back.

"The biggest takeaway is Hank and I are on the same page," I said and moved around the desk to sit down in my chair so I could thumb through the file. As expected, it contained all the information about Etta's case.

"That wasn't one bit interesting." Dottie snorted and gave a good eyeroll. "No fussing? No fighting?"

"Not at all." I shook my head, happy not to be the subject of gossip tonight. "But we do need to talk about what our next step is now that we've talked to Clay."

"Yeah. He actually thought Mae could get Hank to look into Etta's murder, but we somehow got him to let us help," Abby said and opened the notebook. "Let's just go over everything we've gotten."

"Maybe something will be a trigger," I said.

We all dragged over chairs to sit in our familiar semicircle in the office, where we each brought our focus to the list Abby was compiling in her notebook. As her pen skittered across the page, the suspects in Etta's murder took shape in a neat column.

"All right," Abby began, tapping her pen against the lined paper. "First off, we've got Clay, Etta's estranged husband."

"But his alibi seems solid," I pointed out, recalling the receipt he'd shown us from the apartment in Slade.

"He has an alibi," Betts agreed, nodding thoughtfully. "But we need to verify it."

"I can check into that," Agnes chirped, looking like a little canary in her yellow sundress. She was so cute, and I loved how she snuck around Al by funneling information to our group. Now she felt like she was one of us.

"Then there's Keely, Etta's daughter," Abby continued, her brow creased in concentration.

Dottie huffed a laugh. "Honey, I've seen ice cubes with more motive."

I couldn't help but grin at Dottie's remark, but there was truth in her words. Keely seemed genuinely grieved by her mother's death, a poor suspect at best.

"Edna?" Queenie asked cautiously. We all turned to her, knowing full well that Edna was the one person who had been detained by Sheriff Hemmer.

Agnes shook her head vigorously. "Edna didn't do it. I'll stake my pension on it. Al only brought her in because he needed to look like he was doing something."

"That leaves Adrienne," I said, remembering the discomfort that had seeped from the young woman when we'd encountered her at Etta's house.

"And let's not forget Andy, Keely's boyfriend," Betts added, leaning back in her chair. "He seemed to be at odds with Adrienne. Could there be something there?"

"Whoever it is," I said, feeling the weight of the situation settle over us, "they're still out there, and they've got every reason to keep quiet."

In the silence that followed, our resolve solidified. Each of us knew what needed to be done. The killer was hiding in plain sight, and it was up to us to uncover the truth.

Betts, ever the cautious one, squinted at Abby's notebook. "Now, why Adrienne? She seemed right shocked at the news."

I considered this for a moment, recalling the body language between Adrienne and Keely's boyfriend, Andy. "There was a certain tension between Adrienne and Andy, Keely's boyfriend. I can't put my finger on it, but it was palpable."

Abby jumped in, "Adrienne seemed uncomfortable with our presence at the house, particularly after she realized Mae had been asking about Etta and the family earlier at the Cookie Crumble."

"Also, she lived with Keely," Dottie chimed in, "so she'd know about Etta's hoarding, right? She might know about some valuable item Etta had tucked away somewhere."

"Right," Abby said. "And we know Etta trusted Adrienne. She might have even taken her to the shed to show her something in there."

"Or Adrienne knew Etta stored valuable things in that shed and wanted to get her hands on something," I suggested. "But Etta caught her, and Adrienne had to... had to silence her."

Agnes shifted in her chair, her expression serious. "Remember, all these are theories. We can't be accusing folks without solid proof."

There was a moment of silence as we all nodded, understanding the gravity of Agnes's words.

Abby pushed her long ponytail behind her shoulder and looked at the group thoughtfully. "Why would Andy be the killer? Isn't he dating Keely? It wouldn't make much sense for him to hurt her mother."

Betts tapped her fingers on the table thoughtfully. "True, but people have been known to do strange things for love or money."

Dottie chimed in with her Southern drawl, "Well, darlin', if he was trying to get his hands on something valuable from Etta's hoard, then there's the motive. They are college kids after all."

Queenie nodded, adding, "And if Keely and Etta weren't getting along because of her hoarding, maybe Andy saw it as a way to win points with Keely by removing the source of their arguments."

Agnes rubbed her chin thoughtfully. "That's a possibility, but it's still a long shot."

I cleared my throat, ready to contribute to the spitballing. "And there's also the fact that he was not comfortable with Adrienne. There might be something between them we're not aware of. Maybe Andy was trying to cover his tracks."

"Or perhaps he didn't mean for things to end up the way they did." Abby's brow furrowed in concentration. "Maybe they had an argument that escalated."

"Well, whatever the case," Queenie said, "I reckon we have some serious sleuthing ahead of us."

"Etta must've trusted them," Betts surmised, her gaze serious. "Whoever it was, she led them to that shed."

As we poured over the file, our theories and conjectures filled the room, the atmosphere crackling with urgency. As darkness fell outside, we knew our search for truth was far from over.

I pulled out the autopsy report, the paper crinkling in my hands as I unfolded it. Everyone was silent as they leaned closer, their gazes locked on the document.

"Let's see what it says." I scanned the first page. My eyes skimmed the familiar language of an autopsy report, something I'd become accustomed to in my detective work.

I began to read from the coroner's report. "According to Colonel

Holz, Etta Hardgrove, fifty-eight years of age, was found deceased in the yard of her residence. The cause of death is blunt force trauma to the head, which caused a severe brain injury."

I looked up, meeting the somber faces of my friends. Betts had her hand on her mouth, Abby was furiously scribbling notes, Dottie had crossed her arms and was shaking her head, Queenie looked somber, and Agnes had a resigned expression.

"The pathologist also found fragments of concrete in the wound," I continued, feeling my own heart thud in my chest. "Which corroborates what we found in the shed. There were also signs of a struggle. There were abrasions on her hands and knees, dirt under her nails."

Betts gasped softly, "That poor woman."

Abby's pen didn't stop moving as she asked, "What about time of death?"

"According to the report, it was sometime between eight in the morning and noon," I replied.

Dottie clucked her tongue, "In broad daylight during the 127 Yard Sale? That's gutsy."

"It also means there were likely plenty of people around," Agnes pointed out. "We need to find witnesses."

We all nodded in agreement. The more information we had, the better chance we had of figuring out who did this to Etta and why.

"I wonder if Keely was going to work the yard sale for her mother?" Abby asked a good question.

"All the college kiddos I know don't get up that early on a Saturday mornin'." Dottie made a great point. "But that don't mean they didn't do it."

Queenie, who'd been leaning back in her chair thoughtfully, finally spoke up. "What if it was someone passing through for the yard sale?" she suggested. "I mean, we all know Etta was a hard bargainer. She could've taken a particularly interested buyer back to the shed to show them something special and when they couldn't agree on a price..."

She didn't need to finish. We all knew what could have happened next.

Betts shivered. "That's a chilling thought, Queenie."

"But it makes sense," Abby said, still scribbling away. "If it was someone from out of town, they'd have less ties to the community. Less reason to worry about getting caught."

Dottie nodded. "And it would explain why no one local saw anything suspicious. They're used to seeing strangers around during the yard sale."

"But wouldn't there be some sort of evidence left behind?" I asked, playing devil's advocate. "A dropped item, tire tracks, something?"

"We'll have to comb through the case file to see if Al missed anything," Agnes said. "Or maybe even go back to the scene ourselves."

Betts adjusted her glasses and cleared her throat, drawing our attention. "When Abby sent me over to chat with the neighbor, I got the distinct impression she had something to say about the morning of Etta's murder."

"Wait. She was holding out on you?" Abby quirked a brow at Betts.

"It's not that she was withholding information intentionally. We got interrupted. Her son nearly fell off the monkey bars at the park across the street, and she had to rush off to grab him," Betts explained. "Sasha Pitt is her name."

"You think she saw something that morning?" Queenie's eyebrows raised in intrigue.

"I'm almost certain of it," Betts responded firmly. "The way her eyes shifted... and she was biting her lip like she was nervous. I think she was about to share something important."

"We should definitely follow up on that lead." Dottie's Southern drawl pervaded the quiet room. "A neighbor's account could shed some light on this mystery, y'all."

Abby made a note in her book, nodding. Just as Abby closed the notebook, there was a quick knock on the door of the office, then it swung open.

Charlie, the leader of the Camping Cowgirls, peered in with an expectant look on her face. Her hair was in a fancy updo and she was clad in a denim skirt and a plaid shirt, exuding a cowgirl charm.

"Hey there, ladies!" Her smile practically split her face in two. "We're all set up and ready. Can you judge the place setting contest?" She raised her eyebrows with the question, her hand resting on her hip.

We all exchanged a look. Despite the murder investigation occupying our minds, we knew we couldn't let down the Camping Cowgirls. They were my guests, and we owed them a good time. And frankly, a bit of distraction would probably do us some good.

"Sure thing, Charlie," I assured her, rising from my chair. "We wouldn't miss it for the world."

Charlie beamed, clapping her hands together. "Oh, fantastic! Can't wait to see which one you choose. There's some real artistic talent out there, I tell ya!"

With one last glance at the case files on the table, we all followed Charlie out of the office and into the balmy evening air. The potluck was about to begin, and for a little while, we could shift our focus from murder and mayhem to fun and fellowship.

The twilight hue of the Kentucky sky had washed over Happy Trails Campground, silhouetting the vintage campers in all their charming glory. The canvas of stars was just beginning to peek through the soft blush of sunset as the cicadas began their serenade, joined by the occasional croak of a distant frog. Every now and then, a firefly would blink into existence, adding to the magical quality of the evening.

Across the campground, the lake shimmered, reflecting the twinkling lights strung from camper to camper and tree to tree, bathing the space in a warm, welcoming glow.

Within the covered patio of the recreation building, the picnic tables were teeming with life. The Camping Cowgirls mingled, exchanging cheerful banter, while in the background, Blue Ethel and the Adolescent Farm Boys strummed their instruments, their melody melding with the rustling of leaves in the Daniel Boone National Forest bordering the campground.

Dottie and I made our way through the chattering crowd, our task being to judge the place setting contest. Each picnic table was adorned with a different place setting, showcasing the unique style and personality of its creator.

First was an outdoor-themed setting, complete with miniature succulents as the centerpiece and napkins folded into tiny tents.

Next, we spotted a vintage-inspired setting. It boasted delicate china with pastel floral designs paired with intricately knotted lace napkins, all arranged on a crocheted tablecloth that evoked memories of a bygone era.

A fun, kitschy setting caught our eye next; it featured colorful plastic flamingos guarding candy-colored napkins and had a plastic grass skirt for a tablecloth, with tropical drink umbrellas sprinkled across the table.

A southwestern theme graced another table, complete with cacti and desert flowers on a *faux* cowhide tablecloth, while a fifth displayed a modern farmhouse theme with clean lines, neutral tones, and mason jars filled with baby's breath.

As we continued our circuit, one particular table stood out. It was a genuine tribute to cowgirl spirit with a warm, rustic charm. A *faux* wood tablecloth formed the backdrop, while the plates were styled like wagon wheels. The silverware resembled mini branding irons, and the glasses were cleverly designed to mimic cowboy boots. The centerpiece was a stunning arrangement of wildflowers encircled by a miniature lasso. It was the embodiment of the evening's theme, a masterpiece of creativity.

There was no doubt in our minds. "This one is a winner, don't you think?" I asked Dottie, pointing at the cowboy-themed table.

"Sure as sugar, Mae," Dottie affirmed, her eyes sparkling with appreciation. "I reckon we've found our first candidate for winner."

As we looked over the rest, something caught my eye. One place setting was situated at the edge of the crowd, an oasis of iridescent blues and greens that could only be described as a peacock extravaganza.

Feathers served as a show-stopping centerpiece, rising from the table in an impressive plume. The napkins were a deep, jewel-toned teal folded into the shape of a peacock's fan, while the plates shimmered with the same rich hues. But what truly took my breath away were the napkin rings. They were peacock pins, each one a dazzling array of colorful gemstones that mimicked a peacock's plumage.

"Lord Almighty," Dottie gasped beside me, her gaze fixed on the pins. Her voice was a mere whisper, but in the tranquil evening, it carried a weight of realization that sank into my stomach.

My heart pounded in my chest as recognition dawned. There, amidst the glamour of the place setting, was a familiar sight. The peacock pin, identical to the one Etta had showcased at the Tough Nickel but refused to sell. The very same pin Etta had held so dear... now found on what must be Edna's place setting.

The revelation hung in the air, a damning piece of evidence that twisted the narrative we'd been unraveling. The ladies and I exchanged wide-eyed glances, the same thought echoing in our minds.

Could Edna really have had a more sinister role in Etta's untimely demise?

"Mae," Dottie whispered, her voice trembling with the gravity of our discovery. "This... this changes everything." She stepped up and subtly slipped the pin from the table into her pocket.

The revelation of the peacock pin had sent shockwaves through the Laundry Club Ladies. Dottie and I, our minds buzzing with the implications, excused ourselves, leaving the others to continue the festivities while we scoured the group for Edna.

We had some questions for her.

Dottie and I navigated through the maze of retro campers, their twinkling lights casting playful shadows on the gravel pathways. Somewhere in the distance, the croaking of frogs harmonized with the subtle chirping of cicadas. And yet, amidst the serenity of this picturesque campsite, a shadow of unease had settled in.

Dottie broke the silence, her usually buoyant voice weighed down by worry. "Let's check her camper, Mae." Dottie pointed the napkin with Etta's peacock pin in the direction of Edna's vintage camper.

Edna's Airstream gleamed in the moonlight, a silver beacon amidst the vintage campers. It stood out due to its simplicity, a stark contrast to her flamboyant persona. As we neared, the soft glow from inside hinted at its occupant's presence.

Without waiting for us to knock, the door creaked open, revealing Edna. Her eyes were bloodshot, her countenance far from that of the exuberant woman we knew. She looked tired, the excitement of the evening replaced by a crestfallen air.

"Mae, Dottie..." she began, her voice shaking slightly.

"We need to have us a conversation." Dottie took the initiative to step up into the camper, forcing Edna back inside.

Edna looked between Dottie and me, confused, until Dottie held the napkin in the air.

Collapsing onto the camper's small built-in couch, Edna confessed, "After you dropped me at the campground that day, I drove back to the Tough Nickel. Etta was still there, and we had a little chat. And I convinced her to sell me the pin."

As she spoke, she produced a crumpled receipt from her pocket, extending it to us. I took it, scanning the scribbled details. It was indeed a receipt from the Tough Nickel, in Buck's handwriting, dated before Etta's unfortunate end.

Edna had indeed acquired the coveted pin, but the circumstances and timing of the exchange added yet another layer of intrigue to the mystery and how we'd completely gotten it wrong.

Edna definitely didn't appear to be Etta's killer.

At this point, I knew I had to go back to Etta's house and try to pin down the neighbor who had been going to say something to Betts before she had to go rescue her little boy from the monkey bars.

The thought of going back to Etta's house sent a chill down my spine, but if it helped us get to the bottom of her death, it would be worth it.

CHAPTER FIFTEEN

The morning sunlight streamed through the windows of my camper, pulling me from a fitful sleep. I rubbed my eyes, glancing at the clock. Six thirty. With a groan, I stumbled out of the bedroom, grabbing a light sweater to ward off the slight morning chill.

A gentle knock on my camper's door, followed by Hank's familiar, cheerful voice, pulled me fully awake. "Morning, girls," he called through the thin door, referring to me and a very excited Fifi.

The scent of freshly brewed coffee wafted into my nostrils as I pulled open the camper door to Hank's familiar smile. "Morning," he said and smiled, holding a steaming cup extended toward me.

"Good morning," I said, accepting the warm cup and wrapping my hands around it. "You're up early."

I followed Hank to the small table set up under my camper van awning. As I sank into the cushioned chair, Chester and Fifi bounded off, their joyful yips echoing around the campground.

The dawn had painted the sky in hues of pink and orange, the rising sun casting long shadows across the campground. The Daniel Boone National Forest's tree line was softly illuminated, adding a serene backdrop to the already picturesque scene.

Birds were starting to sing, their melodies harmonizing with the soft sounds of the waking campground. The calmness of the moment was soothing, offering a gentle respite from the chaos of the previous day.

Hank sipped his own coffee, his eyes watching the playful dogs. The sunlight caught his face, accentuating the handsome lines etched by years of smiling.

"Preacher Alex messaged this morning," he said, his voice interrupting the peaceful silence. "He wanted to know if we could meet for pie at the diner instead of at the church."

I nodded, already going through my day's plan in my mind.

Hank continued, his eyes now on me, "Still no real leads on the missing teenager case. Just rumors and hearsay, nothing solid to go on." A look of helplessness flashed in his eyes.

I reached out, giving his hand a gentle squeeze.

He looked at me, the corners of his lips curling up into a faint smile. "Thank you, Mae," he murmured. "I assume you have a plan for today?" His hand gently caressed the back of mine.

I nodded, setting down my cup. "After the discovery last night, I think I need to revisit Etta's neighbor. She seemed like she had something to say yesterday before she was interrupted."

Hank's eyebrows raised in interest. "Do you think it's significant?"

"I don't know," I admitted, "but I have a hunch it could be. Besides, it wouldn't hurt to find out."

As I detailed the story of the peacock pin, Edna's confession, and my suspicions, Hank listened intently, occasionally interjecting with his own questions or theories. When I finished, Hank nodded, looking thoughtful. "It does sound odd, a valuable pin at the Tough Nickel, but it could also be a coincidence, you know? Maybe Etta didn't know its worth."

"But what if it's not a coincidence? What if the pin and Etta's murder are connected?"

He took a deep breath, leaning back on his chair. "Okay, let's think this through," he said, running a hand through his hair. "If Etta was murdered for the pin, it could mean the killer knew about its value. But why would they let it end up at a yard sale?"

"Maybe they didn't know she had it until they saw it at the sale," I suggested.

Hank looked at me, considering. "That's a possibility. If they saw it at the sale, they would need to get rid of Etta and retrieve the pin."

"So the murderer could be someone who visited the yard sale."

"That's one theory," Hank agreed. "We should also consider someone close to Etta who knew about the pin. Maybe it wasn't about the pin's monetary value but its sentimental value."

I nodded, turning this new theory over in my mind. "Like a family member or a close friend."

"Exactly. The pin could have been a family heirloom or a memento from a friend. Killing for it could have been driven by emotional motives rather than financial ones."

"Both theories have their merits," I said, taking a sip of my coffee. "I guess we'll just have to dig deeper."

Suddenly, a chill swept across me like a fall breeze had just raced across the lake, though the lake was still, as I recalled my last conversation with Etta.

Hank was quick to notice my shocked expression. "What?"

The lawn chair had belonged to the matriarch of the family, a woman named Clara. She was a tough old bird, known throughout the county for her wit and her moonshine. I remembered word for word what Etta had told us about the lawn chair Dottie had picked up at Etta's curb alert.

Now, as I sat with Hank, the memory of Etta's story felt like a heavy weight. Etta had been killed, and she'd had a lawn chair that had once belonged to Clara Benson. A lawn chair that was supposed to have a value far beyond what most would think.

"Etta had a story about that chair, Hank," I murmured, pulling my gaze away from the morning sun peeking over the tree line to look at him. "She said it belonged to a woman named Clara Benson. Someone known for her wit and moonshine." Something tugged at my soul.

Hank raised an eyebrow. "Interesting combination."

"I think I need to look into this Clara and the possible value of that chair," I said, feeling a new surge of determination. "Who knows? Maybe it's not as innocent as it seems."

The sun continued its climb, the rays growing stronger, chasing away the morning chill. The campground started to stir with the sounds of awakening life—the rustling of leaves, the distant murmurs of waking campers, and the soft lapping of lake waters.

"We have a long day ahead," I said, glancing at Hank.

He nodded, offering a reassuring smile.

"I'm going to wait to go to Etta's house and try to figure out what I can about that lawn chair's original owner. Then, I will meet you for lunch."

"Where do you want to go?"

"Since you're busy with the investigation for the missing teen, why don't we just meet by your office at the Normal Diner?" I suggested. "And we might get to see your sister. I've missed Ellis and Ty since they moved." Ellis and Ty had been full-time RVers until they bought their new house near Abby and Bobby Ray.

"I'm still shocked at how well she's taking to married life and being an instant mother figure." Hank snorted and pushed up to stand. "But you're right. We are busy—and don't be going and getting in trouble," he warned as he walked over to give me a quick kiss.

"Y'all ain't married yet!" I heard Dottie scream as she sauntered down the campground with the feathers of her sheer pink housecoat flapping, hair still curled tight in pink sponges. "Stop that," she fussed at Chester and Fifi, who were both trying to bite at the feathers as though Dottie were a bird for them to play with.

"Come on, boy!" Hank finally called for Chester now that he was halfway down to his fifth wheel.

"Won't be too long till he won't have to leave you to go back to his place." Dottie looked over at my cup.

"The whole pot is brewed." I pointed back to the camper van, even though the cup I had was from Hank. "Help yourself, and bring out the pot."

While Dottie went inside to get coffee, I sat with the thought of the lawn chair in my head and wondered if Dottie knew anything about it.

"Dottie, remember what Etta said about your lawn chair being valuable?" I asked after she came out and refilled my mug.

"Yep." Dottie eased down and took a sip from her mug.

"You got that from a curb alert, and apparently it's worth money." I started to spit out some ideas. "What if someone at the estate sale came to see Etta because they knew she'd gotten the chairs? She did say it was Clara Benson's."

"Yep. Clara Benson had that big ole estate, and she got all her money from moonshining." Dottie snorted. "I wish we had some to put in here."

"I'd like to see you on moonshine." My brows rose at the thought. "I wonder if we can get ahold of someone in her family?"

"I guess you could call her son, Orville. He comes to the Tough Nickel a lot for his antiques." Dottie batted a cigarette out of her case.

"Wait. Orville Benson?" I gasped. "Orville *Jenson*."

"What are you doin'?" Dottie asked.

The revelations were tumbling into my head like a spilled bag of marbles, rolling around and sending me into a frenzy of thoughts. I took a sip of coffee, feeling the warm liquid slide down my throat as I gathered my wits. Dottie, perched on her cushioned stool, leaned back, a cigarette dangling from her fingers, her eyes fixed on me with bemused interest.

"Clara Benson," I repeated, mulling over Dottie's words. "Clara Benson, Orville's mother. Etta said she was known for her wit and moonshine."

Dottie chuckled. "She sure was. That moonshine made her a fortune. Then she turned around and invested in real estate, bought up half of Lebanon."

"And she owned that lawn chair of yours," I added. "Orville, her son, comes to the Tough Nickel a lot for his antiques, you said?"

"Yep, that's what I said. Orville Benson..." Dottie's voice trailed off as her eyes went wide. The cigarette almost slipped from her fingers. "Well, I'll be darned."

An icy shiver ran down my spine. "It has to be the same Orville that Clay and Keely mentioned." My mind raced. "But they called him Orville Jenson, not Benson. Did they get his name wrong, or did he give them a wrong name?"

Dottie's eyes narrowed. "You think he was after my lawn chair? Or should I say, his mama's lawn chair?"

"Think about it, Dottie," I said, my heart hammering. "He's an antiques dealer. He'd know the value of those chairs. Maybe he wanted them back. Maybe he came to Etta's yard sale to get them."

Dottie frowned, her face scrunching up. "But wouldn't he just buy them? Why kill Etta?"

"Maybe things didn't go as planned." I shrugged, trying to make sense of the tangled knot we were slowly unraveling. "We need to talk to Orville. Find out what he knows."

Dottie nodded slowly, her eyes wide. "Well, ain't that something. I never thought my old lawn chair could cause such a ruckus."

I let out a soft sigh, my fingers tightening around my mug. "Let's just hope we can get ahold of Orville and figure out what's really going on." The sun was high in the sky now, casting long shadows over Happy Trails Campground. And with each passing moment, the mystery of Etta's death seemed to grow only deeper.

I'd barely taken my last gulp of coffee when Dottie abruptly rose from the picnic table, her eyes ablaze with that unmistakable fire I'd come to associate with an imminent adventure.

"Mae," she announced, smacking the top of the table, making Fifi jump. "Get up. We're going to Lebanon."

"Lebanon?" I questioned, surprised at the suddenness. "Now?"

"We're not going to get any answers sitting around here," she stated matter-of-factly.

"But don't you think it would be better if we—" I began, but she cut me off.

"And we're going undercover."

"Undercover?" I gaped at her, blinking rapidly. "Dottie, this isn't a spy movie."

"Well, we can't just walk up to Orville and start interrogating him. We need to be subtle. Besides, it'll be fun!" She grinned at me, her excitement infectious. Before I knew it, I found myself agreeing. "I'll go tell Henry to watch the campground, and you go change then pick me up."

I couldn't help but chuckle at Dottie's zest. If nothing else, our escapades were never boring. "All right, Dottie. Let's go undercover."

CHAPTER SIXTEEN

I t took Dottie and me just over two hours to make the journey to Lebanon, passing through rolling Kentucky hills, dense woodlands dotted with limestone outcrops, and an array of small, sleepy towns that seemed to be caught in a time warp.

At last, we found ourselves pulling up outside Orville's Antiques. It was a quaint establishment nestled between two taller, newer buildings, making it look like a holdover from a bygone era. The sign hanging above the entrance was a faded wood, the letters in "Orville's Antiques" hand-painted with an artisan's care, the gold leaf weathered and worn but still retaining a touch of its former glory.

The shop front itself was an endearing mix of old-world charm and vintage eccentricity. Display windows on either side of the doorway showcased an array of items from porcelain dolls and aged, leather-bound books to brass telescopes and intricate, hand-carved wooden furniture. Each item was carefully arranged to tempt passersby with the lure of the past's hidden treasures.

The building was made of red brick that had weathered to a soft rose hue over the decades, and the roof was lined with a row of dormer windows, hinting at a spacious upper floor. Hanging baskets filled with trailing ivy and vibrant red geraniums added a splash of color, softening the building's edges.

"Well, here we are," I said, looking over at Dottie as we sat in the car, taking a moment to appraise our destination.

Her eyes gleamed behind her oversized sunglasses. "Let's go see what Mr. Orville Benson has to say for himself."

The clang of a bell echoed in the hushed interior as I pushed the door open, ushering us into a trove of antiques. The scent of polished wood, old books, and a hint of dust filled my nose as I took in the sight. Stacked to the rafters, the shop was a labyrinth of treasures, each item bearing the patina of history.

A worn Persian rug softened the creaking hardwood floor beneath our feet as we made our way past a mahogany desk studded with ink pots, an ornate Victorian mirror that reflected a past era, and rows of glass cabinets displaying a menagerie of porcelain figurines, tarnished silver cutlery, and delicately painted tea sets. In one corner, a gramophone with a gleaming brass horn held court while a grandfather clock ticked away, its slow rhythm punctuating the quiet murmur of hushed conversations.

"Don't you just love antiques!" Dottie trilled as she strolled into the shop, her large hat wobbling on her head with each step. I held back a chuckle at the sight of us. We must've looked like we stepped straight out of a 1960s spy movie.

An employee, a young man who looked barely out of high school, glanced up from the counter. His eyes widened at the sight of Dottie, swathed in her dramatic disguise. "Um, can I help you with anything in particular?"

Dottie swooped over to a glass case filled with delicate porcelain figurines. "Oh, aren't these just exquisite?" she exclaimed, her fingers hovering dangerously close to a delicate Dresden ballerina, its hand-painted face etched with a demure smile.

The employee rushed over, alarmed. "Please, ma'am, be careful. That figurine is very valuable."

Meanwhile, I took advantage of the distraction Dottie was creating.

I roamed the shop's aisles, eyeing each item I passed with interest—that was, until something in the corner of the room caught my attention. A vintage lawn chair, remarkably similar to Dottie's, rested against an old wooden bookshelf, its metal frame gleaming under the shop's soft light.

I sidled up to the chair, keeping one eye on Dottie, who was now theatrically admiring an ornate, gilded mirror, and the other on the chair. The design, the material, even the slight rust on the hinges—it was all too familiar. A shiver ran down my spine. This had to be more than just a coincidence.

If I knew antique dealers, they always liked having a complete pair or set of things to increase the value, and it looked as though he only had one here. Which would give him motive to try to get Etta to sell him back the lawn chair that Etta had bought from his mother's estate.

Just as I was about to reach out to touch the chair, a voice behind me interrupted my thoughts. "That's a fine piece, isn't it?"

I turned around to face an older man with a warm smile, his eyes twinkling behind round spectacles.

He extended a hand. "I'm Orville, the owner of this fine establishment."

Over his shoulder, I witnessed a lively commotion at the far end of the shop, unmistakably Dottie. She was in the midst of an exaggerated display of enthusiasm over an intricately decorated teapot. The employee attending her was growing visibly nervous, especially when she lifted the precious item for closer examination.

Before I could intervene, Orville's gaze was drawn to the spectacle, a slow grin spreading across his face. "Dottie? Is that you?" he asked.

So much for undercover. Dottie had neglected to mention she knew Orville.

Dottie whirled around, her face splitting into a grin as she recognized Orville. She waddled over to us, practically throwing herself at Orville. "Oh, Orville, you old coot! How long has it been?"

He chuckled, wrapping an arm around her. "Too long, Dottie, too long." He paused, a gleam in his eyes. "Do you remember that one time at Happy Trails when Harrison fell into the lake trying to catch that big catfish?"

Dottie let out a raucous laugh. "Oh heavens! I'll never forget the look on his face!"

I stood there, a little stunned at the familiar banter. "So you know each other?"

Orville nodded, a reminiscent smile on his face. "Oh yes. Harrison was my best friend. We had some grand times at Happy Trails back in the day. Never a dull moment with that man around, I tell you."

I could see how fond he was of Dottie's deceased husband, Harrison, and the memories they'd shared.

I watched as Orville chuckled and clapped Dottie on the shoulder, his gaze twinkling with mischief.

"Dottie, you always did have a knack for finding the most interesting pieces. What are you doing two hours away from home today?" he asked.

Dottie feigned a gasp, clutching at her heart. "Well, sugar, I got my hands on something you might just be interested in. Do you remember those grand lawn chairs of Clara's?"

At the mention of the lawn chairs, Orville's eyes widened a touch, but his smile didn't fade.

"Clara's chairs? Well, I'll be. Mama loved those chairs. They were quite the item back in the day. In fact, your friend here was just looking at one." He glanced my way.

"Now, don't you go getting any wild ideas." Dottie wagged her finger at him, her voice filled with teasing. "I got one of those chairs from Etta Hardgrove, and she's ended up dead. You wouldn't be killin' ladies over lawn furniture now, would ya, Orville?" She reached over and smacked his arm lightly, her laughter tinkling through the shop.

Orville's laugh joined hers, the sound rich and deep. But behind his glasses, I noticed a brief flicker in his eyes, a momentary shadow.

Could it be guilt, or was it just the mention of Etta's tragic end? My mind was spinning with possibilities as I watched their reunion continue.

Orville's eyes crinkled at the corners, his laughter still filling the room. "Dottie, you have always been a hoot! Kill over lawn chairs? I wouldn't dream of it." He shook his head, a wide grin spread across his face.

He grew more serious then, his tone taking on a more thoughtful air. "Clara's chairs hold fond memories, sure, but they're not really my style. Too much... frill. It's her painting collection that I've always been partial to. Now that, I might just be willing to do some desperate things for," he said with a wink. "No, I've been busy trying to get my hands on some new pieces down at an antique show in Georgia. Just got back in town, in fact. Heard about Etta though."

His voice lowered, the jovial tone replaced by a genuine note of regret. "She and I used to chat on the phone often, discussing the trade. I've tried countless times to buy some of her jewelry, but she always refused. Stubborn as a mule, that one." He looked around, suddenly appearing thoughtful. "So who do I need to talk to about her pieces now? Surely someone is taking care of them?"

His sincerity seemed to dissolve any lingering suspicion I had. It was clear that Etta and Orville had a genuine connection, one formed over a shared passion for antiques.

"You can contact her husband or daughter," I offered. "I believe they're selling much of her collection."

Orville nodded, his face softening. "Etta was a good woman. A tough nut to crack, but with a heart of gold. She didn't deserve such a fate."

Dottie, who'd been quiet for a moment, cleared her throat. "Well, Orville, we just wanted to check up on you and clear up any... misunderstandings," she said, ending with a theatrical flutter of her eyelashes.

Orville laughed again, a deep, rich sound that echoed around the store. "Always straight to the point, aren't you, Dottie? Well, I appreciate the visit. And the chair? I'm glad it found a good home."

He walked us to the door, giving each of us a firm handshake. As we climbed back into my little Ford, I looked at Dottie. She seemed deep in thought, and I decided to break the silence.

"Well, that's one person checked off the list, Dottie," I said, turning the engine on.

She nodded slowly, her gaze still on the antiques store as we drove away. "Yes, and a whole lot more to go."

Her words hung in the air as we left Lebanon, heading back toward Happy Trails Campground. The mystery of Etta's death was far from over, but one thing was certain. We wouldn't rest until we found the truth.

CHAPTER SEVENTEEN

The familiar aroma of the Normal Diner washed over me as Hank and I stepped through the front door. It was an intoxicating blend of brewing coffee, sizzling bacon, and the slightly sweet scent of maple syrup that always seemed to linger in the air. The diner was coming to life for the lunch rush, with the usual crowd claiming their favorite booths and counter spots.

Hank slid into a booth across from me, his gaze taking in the room before resting on the laminated menu in his hands. I followed his gaze, my own fingers tracing the familiar outlines of the lunch specials, my stomach grumbling in response.

The Normal Diner was a staple in our town, known for its hearty home-cooked meals and freshly brewed coffee. The walls were adorned with an eclectic mix of vintage posters and local artwork, while the counter was lined with red leather stools that spun in squeaky circles. A large jukebox nestled in the corner, crooning out tunes from another era.

Ty Randal approached our table with a welcoming smile. He and Hank had a brief conversation about the house and Ellis. He quickly filled our mugs with the diner's rich, dark-roast coffee. "I'll be right back. I just took a fresh apple pie out of the oven." Ty hurried off.

Preacher Alex hadn't arrived yet, but I knew he wouldn't be far off.

Hank took a slow sip of his coffee, his eyes meeting mine over the rim of his mug. I could see the worry lines around his eyes and knew that, like me, he was mulling over the events of the past days. The conversation with Orville, the continuing mystery surrounding Etta's murder, the missing teenager, and our own personal issues were taking a toll on us both.

"Now what are you going to do?" Hank asked.

"I guess I'm going to go see Etta's neighbor this afternoon and see if she was going to tell Betts anything before she was interrupted." I sighed. "What about your case?"

"The lead I thought was going somewhere? It was a dead end." He shook his head in defeat. "But I will find her."

There was no doubt in my mind Hank wouldn't. It was just a matter of when.

The door chime rang again, the comforting sound easily heard over the hum of the diner's busy afternoon activities. I glanced up, my eyes immediately catching sight of Preacher Alex as he stepped inside. He paused, his eyes scanning the diner for our table.

Hank noticed, too, lifting a hand high into the air.

"Over here, Alex!" he called out, grinning as the preacher's gaze landed on us.

He made his way over, weaving through the crowd with an ease that suggested he was a regular. He slid into the booth across from us. "No sooner than I sit down, here's Ty," Alex chuckled as Ty came to our table.

"Alex! How's it going?" Ty asked with a wide grin, shaking hands with the preacher.

"All good, Ty. How about that Turkey Run we talked about? We doing it this fall?" Preacher Alex returned the handshake with enthusiasm. He had a booming, friendly voice that immediately commanded attention.

Ty laughed, scratching his head. "If you can convince my knees. Ellis has got me switching out the carpet in the house to that vinyl flooring."

"Well, I have been known to work miracles," Preacher Alex joked, his eyes twinkling with good-natured humor. Their banter brought a light-hearted moment amidst our heavy thoughts.

Ty turned to us next. "What about you two? Got anyone to set our handsome preacher here up with?"

He winked at Preacher Alex, his eyebrows wagging suggestively.

Hank snorted, nearly spitting out his coffee, while I felt my cheeks heat up.

"Ty!" I gasped, unsure if I should be amused or mortified.

Ty just shrugged, his grin undiminished. "Just trying to help a brother out."

"And I am a man." Alex lifted his hand in gesture.

We all burst out laughing then, the tension at our table lifting for a brief moment. The laughter echoed around the familiar sounds of the diner—the clinking of silverware, the sizzle of food on the griddle, and the chatter of our fellow patrons.

It was a comforting soundtrack to our meeting, as I wondered what would come from laying it all out on the line so Alex Elliott could decide whether he thought Hank and I should get married. *Who ever heard of such?* I looked over at him. All joking aside, the man didn't have a girlfriend, so why did I even agree to do this?

For the moment, I decided it was just us, friends gathered together amidst the warm aroma of coffee and the glow of the afternoon sunlight streaming through the diner windows.

That was it.

Until it wasn't. Then the questions would start to fly.

Preacher Alex ordered a slice of cherry pie from Ty, his gaze momentarily fixed on the dessert display as Ty jotted down the order. When Ty had left us, he leaned back, looking from me to Hank with a thoughtful expression.

"I felt that our first conversation was good, and you both seem to be on the right path," he began, steepling his fingers in front of him. "However, I wanted us to meet here, somewhere casual and comfortable, to discuss living arrangements. It's one of the aspects of marriage that can lead to a lot of misunderstandings if not addressed properly. And from what y'all were saying the other night, I'm not so sure you're on the same page."

Hank nodded, taking a sip from his coffee mug.

I held onto my own, the warmth seeping into my palms. I knew this topic was going to come up eventually. Hank and I had been tiptoeing around it since we'd gotten engaged.

"Now, Mae," Alex continued, turning to me. "You love your camper van, it's clear. It's your home, your sanctuary. But have you considered the practicalities of sharing such a small space long-term?"

I nodded, playing with the handle of my mug. I'd heard this song and dance before from Mary Elizabeth. "I have. It's perfect for one person, maybe even two if we're just traveling. But as a long-term living solution... I know it might not be ideal," I confessed.

He smiled, acknowledging my honesty. "And Hank, what about your fifth wheel? How do you feel about Mae moving in?"

Hank was silent for a moment before answering. "I'd love for Mae to move in. But it's not just about what I want. It's her home too."

We shared a look then, a silent conversation passing between us. The truth was, we both loved the campground, loved the freedom of being close to nature. We'd been living our separate lives in our own spaces, but if we were going to make a go of this, some changes were needed.

"Mae, do you know what you want?" Preacher Alex asked me point-blank.

Just as I was about to answer Preacher Alex's question, I cocked my head to one side and squinted at him suspiciously. "Hold on, did Mary Elizabeth put you up to this?" I accused, pointing a finger at him.

Hank choked on his coffee, coughing as he tried to contain his laughter.

"Excuse me?" Preacher Alex looked shocked, but I saw a hint of laughter dancing in his eyes.

"She's been going on and on about wanting grandbabies," I persisted.

"And you know as well as I do that my camper van isn't exactly baby-friendly."

"Mae, that's..." Hank began, but I waved him off.

Preacher Alex laughed outright then, leaning back in his chair. "No, Mae, Mary Elizabeth didn't put me up to this. But you have to admit, a fifth wheel does offer more room for, let's say, expansion."

He was lying! I could tell by him shifting in his seat that Mary Elizabeth must've promised him something for the church.

Hank's chuckles subsided as he nudged me. "He's got a point, darlin'."

"Expansion, huh?" I echoed, shaking my head. "This is Mary Elizabeth's doing, I can feel it. Did she promise you something, preacher? Maybe an extra collection of children's Bibles for Sunday School?"

For a moment, Preacher Alex looked like he'd been caught. He cleared his throat, avoiding my eyes, then finally came out with the truth. "Well, the church could use some more children's Bibles, and as it happens, Mary Elizabeth did offer to..."

"That's it!" I said, pointing triumphantly at him. "I knew it."

Despite my accusations, the mood remained light. After a moment, I relented, turning to Hank and squeezing his hand. "I love my camper van. It's part of who I am. But... I love Hank more. And if moving into his fifth wheel makes our life together more comfortable, then I'm willing to do that."

"I believe that's a step in the right direction," the preacher said.

And with that, Ty arrived with Preacher Alex's pie, and I looked forward to shifting the conversation to less daunting topics, knowing we'd made some real progress.

But first, Preacher Alex clapped his hands together vigorously before he dug into the pie. "I can't wait to get those new children's Bibles," he teased.

CHAPTER EIGHTEEN

I pulled up to the park near Etta's neighborhood, the low hum of chatter from the 127 Yard Sale buzzing in the distance. I noticed a lot of empty tables. The annual miles-long yard sale was nearing its end, and it was slim pickings at this point.

The park across the street from Etta's house was alive with mothers and their children. I scanned the park, my gaze landing on a woman who matched Betts' description of Sasha Pitt.

I pulled my little Ford into the next parking spot along the road. With my eyes set on Sasha, I walked down the road toward the park. The yard sale tables that had been in front of Etta's house before were now gone. There weren't any cars in her driveway.

I darted left and right, trying to get out of the way of the children playing tag and using me as a buffer.

"Don't run the lady over!" yelled one of the mothers standing next to Sasha.

"It's fine. No harm, no foul," I said, offering them a friendly smile. "Are you Sasha?"

"Yes, can I help you?" Her eyes were wary as she held her young son in her arms.

"I'm Mae, a friend of Etta Hardgrove. I was wondering if we could talk about Etta?" I asked.

Her face softened. "Of course," she said.

We settled onto a nearby bench, the park a symphony of children's laughter and chatter from the mothers. As Sasha began to share her memories, her eyes gazed out toward Etta's house, a soft smile playing at her lips.

"Well, there was this one time... My boy, Alfie, he must've been three or four," she began, a fond glint in her eyes. "He had this toy car he was obsessed with. One day he was playing with it in the yard, and it rolled away right down the street. Alfie was devastated."

A few other mothers close enough to hear smiled and nodded. Some of them frowned, as though they were remembering poor Etta's fate.

Sasha chuckled softly. "And there was Etta, sipping iced tea on her porch. She saw the whole thing. Without missing a beat, she got up, walked down the street, picked up the car, and brought it back to him. You would've thought she'd handed him the moon, the way he lit up."

I smiled, picturing the scene.

"And another time," Sasha continued, her smile broadening, "we had a particularly nasty storm. There was a power outage, and Alfie was scared of the dark. And who do you think showed up at our door with a flashlight and a pack of glow sticks? Etta."

Her story of Etta being a little peculiar caused us to cackle more.

Sasha laughed, shaking her head. "She sat with us, told Alfie stories about how darkness was just a canvas for our imagination, how we could fill it with whatever we wanted. Alfie wasn't scared after that."

Sasha paused for a moment. "Etta was good to us," she finally said, her voice filled with a warm gratitude. "A little eccentric, sure. Her house filled with all sorts of things she collected. But she was kind, a steady presence. And she was very protective of all of us. Especially the women in the neighborhood."

Suddenly, the voices around us fell silent, replaced by the growl of a U-Haul truck pulling up and stopping in Etta's driveway.

Clay hopped out, his eyes scanning the area before landing on Etta's house. A line of cars pulled up behind him, and out stepped Keely, Adrienne, and Andy.

Some of the mothers around us stood, their interest piqued too. The park had turned into a spectator stand. There were whispers and hushed voices as they watched the scene unfold.

"He's here a lot," one mother murmured. "Etta never did like him much, you know."

"Who? Andy?" My ears had perked up at the comment, my detective instincts kicking in. "Why do you say that?" I asked, trying to keep my voice casual.

"Oh, you know. Etta was always one to speak her mind," the other mother shrugged. "She said he acted like he ruled Keely. Used to make comments about it. It didn't sit well with Etta, that's for sure."

I filed that away, watching as Clay and Keely disappeared into the back of the U-Haul carrying all sorts of things from the house. Soon after, Adrienne and Andy came out of the house carrying stacks of boxes.

Another mom spoke up. "Apparently, she didn't care much for that one either."

"Which one?" I asked, not sure if she was talking about Adrienne or Andy or Keely. All three of them had emerged from the U-Haul and headed back toward the house.

"Not Keely. Her friend." The woman pointed her chin across the street and picked up her daughter. The little girl cupped her hand over her mama's ear and whispered loud enough for us to hear that she had to use the bathroom.

"If you'll excuse us," the mama said with pride as though her daughter had used polite manners. It was the same look Mary Elizabeth would get when I was a teenager and did something she liked.

Though I had more questions about why Etta didn't like Adrienne or Andy, our conversation got interrupted when Keely came out of the house and jumped back in the U-Haul as Clay drove them off.

"She was there that morning." Another mom pointed out Adrienne.

"That morning?" I asked, remembering Adrienne telling me she'd worked at the Cookie Crumble. "Do you know what time?"

"It was early. Before the rooster crowed." She snorted before she was called away by her child, who'd just been down the slide and was trying to rub out a slide burn.

I peeled myself away from the group of chattering moms and strode across the lawn, my heart pounding in my chest. Adrienne was a few paces away, her back to me, overseeing the loading of boxes into the car.

I walked up to her, stopping a few feet away. I took a deep breath, bracing myself. "Adrienne," I said, my voice steady.

She turned around, her eyes wide in surprise. "Mae? What are you doing here?" she asked, nervously adjusting her hold on the box in her arms.

"I should ask you the same thing. I thought you said you worked at Cookie Crumble that morning." My gaze was steady, and I saw a flicker of panic cross her face.

"I... I was here early. Before work," she stammered out and headed back to the house.

I stalked in behind her and followed her to the family room, where a lot stuff had been cleared out. "But you didn't mention that before, did you?" I asked, a pit forming in my stomach, touching her to get her to stop walking.

She turned. She swallowed hard, not meeting my gaze.

Just then, her phone chimed from her pocket. Without thinking, she pulled it out to check the message. My eyes caught a glimpse of Clay's name on the screen before she quickly hid it.

A surge of realization hit me, and all the pieces fell into place.

"Adrienne, have you been seeing Clay?" I asked, my voice barely above a whisper.

She looked up at me, her eyes wide with fear. "He... he wasn't happy with Etta, Mae. He said he was trapped. We started talking and things just... happened." Her voice was shaking, her face pale. Before long,

Adrienne was sobbing, her body shuddering with the weight of her confession.

I found myself a mix of emotions, but there was one question that continued to nag me. "How did this even start, Adrienne? Clay and you...?" My own voice was shaky.

Adrienne wiped her eyes, a miserable look on her face. "It... it was a while back. Clay would drop by at the university, unannounced, to see Keely. Sometimes, she would be in class or with Andy..."

I stood facing the window and saw the U-Haul had pulled back into the drive. There was no way they'd gotten too far down the road.

"We would talk about... everything, really. He started opening up to me about his frustrations with Etta... her hoarding... how he felt trapped. He said he couldn't breathe, Mae," Adrienne confessed, her eyes filled with pain. "He felt alone. And I... I was lonely too."

Her words hit me like a punch. The betrayal wasn't just Adrienne's or Clay's. It was a festering wound that had begun long before the murder.

I saw Keely getting out of the passenger side of the truck and decided to keep Adrienne talking. "And so... you two started seeing each other," I said, my voice cold.

Adrienne nodded, more tears streaming down her face. "I know it was wrong, Mae. But... but we found comfort in each other. It wasn't supposed to be like this... I never wanted anyone to get hurt."

The heaviness of her confession was crushing. Clay's infidelity, Adrienne's guilt, Etta's murder—all of it was too much to digest.

The sound of Keely's footsteps echoed in my ears, a haunting reminder of the damage that had been done. Only Adrienne didn't seem to hear anyone coming, so I kept her talking. "Does Keely know?" I asked, my mind racing.

"She doesn't. Etta found out. She threatened to tell Keely, and I... I panicked." Tears streamed down her face, and I watched as she crumbled under the weight of it all.

I reached for my phone to dial Al's number, knowing there was no turning back. The truth had come out, and with it, a whirlwind of heartbreak and pain.

Adrienne couldn't stop the flood of confession. "I followed Etta to the shed that morning. She wouldn't stop talking about telling Keely. She handed me that concrete statue to take to the sale. I... I lost it, Mae." Her voice was a broken whisper, her words echoing in the silence.

I felt my heart drop, my hands shaking as I tried to find Al's contact in my phone.

"I hit her, Mae. Twice. I didn't know what to do. I put the statue back, and I left." Adrienne's final words hung in the air between us, a chilling revelation that left me speechless.

Adrienne didn't appear to be in her body. She didn't even appear to see me holding my phone or Keely standing in the doorway, hearing her best friend confess to having killed her mama.

Before I could say anything else, Keely's gasp rang out behind us. Adrienne whipped around to see Keely there, her face pale, her eyes wide with shock. Clay stood next to her, his expression one of complete disbelief.

CHAPTER NINETEEN

The sun was just starting to dip below the horizon as I sat by the campfire with Betts, Abby, Queenie, and Dottie. The flames flickered and crackled, casting dancing shadows on our faces.

The Camping Cowgirls were hitching up their adorable vintage campers, ready to hit the road after another fun-filled weekend at Happy Trails Campground. Their laughter and chatter filled the air, but a heaviness hung around our little group.

I had gathered everyone to tell them about the day's events, about the painful confession that had ended with Al handcuffing Adrienne and leading her away. There was a hush as I began to speak. "So, it was Adrienne all along," I said, the words tasting bitter in my mouth.

Betts had an arm around Abby, and Queenie was leaning on Dottie's shoulder.

"Adrienne was having an affair with Clay," I continued, the details tumbling out of me. "She thought Etta was going to tell Keely. She panicked and... and she hit Etta."

We all stared into the fire as I told them how Adrienne had confessed to killing Etta, how she'd used one of the concrete statues from Etta's shed. I told them about Keely's shocked gasp when she overheard Adrienne's confession.

There was a collective gasp around the fire. Abby clung tighter to Betts, her face pale. Queenie muttered a prayer under her breath, and Dottie was uncharacteristically silent, her face solemn.

"And Clay?" Queenie finally asked, her voice low.

"He confessed as well," I said. "Apparently, she'd called him right after... after it happened. He helped her cover it up. He was the one who moved Etta's body to the shed."

As the news sank in, the atmosphere was thick with disbelief and sadness. But life, as it always did, continued around us.

The Camping Cowgirls waved as they drove off in their line of vintage campers, the last of the daylight reflecting off their painted surfaces. As we waved back, a melancholy silence fell over us, the fire crackling the only sound in the fading light.

Etta was gone, the mystery of her murder solved, but in its wake was left a trail of heartbreak and betrayal.

Just as the last of the vintage campers turned a corner and disappeared from sight, I cleared my throat, drawing the attention of the others. The glow of the bonfire painted their curious faces in hues of orange and gold.

"I have some other news," I said, swallowing hard against the knot in my throat. "Hank and I... We've decided that Fifi and I are going to move into his fifth wheel after we get married. With him and Chester, I mean."

There was a beat of stunned silence before Dottie broke it. Her loud, boisterous laugh rang out through the campgrounds, startling a bird from its perch in a nearby tree.

"Well, I'll be! What about your camper van?" Dottie asked.

"The camper van will stay right here," I said, unable to keep the smile from my face. "We can use it as a rental just like the others."

Betts and Abby laughed while Queenie just shook her head, a wide grin playing on her lips. "Never a dull moment with you, Mae," she said.

"As for you, Dottie," I said, meeting the older woman's gaze head-on to remind her about the ancient but fancy lawn chair she'd dragged over to the fire. "You owe me a moonshine."

"No time for resting on your laurels, Mae! We'll do plenty of drinkin' soon." Dottie shot up from her chair, her eyes twinkling with mischief under the starlit sky. "You better go pack your bags."

I blinked at her in confusion, my smile slowly giving way to a puzzled frown. "Pack my bags? Dottie, what are you talking about?"

Dottie crossed her arms over her chest, looking as proud as a peacock. "Did you think we were going to let you get hitched without a proper send-off?" Her grin widened at my stunned expression. "We're whisking you away for your bachelorette party!"

"What?" I echoed, my voice a squeaky whisper. My mind was a whirlwind of confusion. "A bachelorette party?"

But as I glanced around at the faces of my friends all lit up with excitement, I couldn't help but laugh. I should have known they'd have something up their sleeves.

"Hank is busy with his missing person case, so we will keep you occupied," Dottie noted.

"Well, then," I said, standing up and brushing the dirt from my jeans. "I suppose I'd better go pack. Can't keep my party waiting."

As Dottie ushered me toward my camper with a whoop of excitement, I couldn't help but shake my head, my heart full. Whatever my bachelorette party had in store for me, with these women by my side, I knew it was going to be a night to remember.

"And one more thing," Dottie called after me, her grin practically audible in her voice. "We're taking your camper van!"

I stopped in my tracks, swiveling around to stare at her. "We're what?"

Dottie chuckled, her eyes glinting under the moonlight. "You heard me, honey. Your precious Fifi's going to have to stay here. We figured it would be fitting for your last 'single' adventure."

That drew a laugh out of me, my earlier surprise melting into amusement. "All right then," I said, shaking my head.

"We are leaving in the morning," Betts called out. "Go get a good night's sleep."

With one last glance back at the group, their faces bright with anticipation, I headed toward my camper. I could already tell this was going to be a trip unlike any other.

Even as the quiet hush of the night descended around me, the campground alive with the gentle rustling of trees and the distant hoot of an owl, I could still hear their excited chatter. I couldn't help but smile, anticipation bubbling within me.

My bachelorette party. In my camper van. With the most wonderful group of women I had ever known.

What could possibly go wrong?

THE END

If you enjoyed reading this book as much as I enjoyed writing it then be sure to return to the Amazon page and leave a review.

Go to Tonyakappes.com for a full reading order of my novels and while there join my newsletter. You can also find links to Facebook, Instagram and Goodreads.

Continue your adventure at the Happy Trails Campground . #33 Witness, Woods, & Wedding is now available to purchase or in Kindle Unlimited.

RECIPES AND CAMPING HACKS FROM MAE WEST AND THE
LAUNDRY CLUB LADIES AT THE HAPPY TRAILS CAMPGROUND
IN NORMAL KENTUCKY.

Campfire Chili Cheese Fries

Enjoy this hearty and flavorful campfire meal!

Ingredients:

- 4 large potatoes, washed and sliced into fries
- 1 pound ground beef or turkey
- 1 onion, diced
- 2 cloves garlic, minced
- 1 can (14 ounces) diced tomatoes
- 1 can (15 ounces) kidney beans, drained and rinsed
- 1 tablespoon chili powder
- 1 teaspoon cumin
- Salt and pepper to taste
- Shredded cheddar cheese
- Green onions, sliced (optional)
- Sour cream (optional)

Instructions:

1. Prepare your campfire and let the flames die down to hot coals.
2. Place a cast iron skillet or a heavy-duty aluminum foil tray on a grill grate over the fire.
3. In the skillet, cook the ground beef or turkey, breaking it up into crumbles, until browned. Add the diced onion and minced garlic, and cook until the onion is translucent.
4. Stir in the diced tomatoes with their juices, kidney beans, chili powder, cumin, salt, and pepper. Let the mixture simmer for about 10-15 minutes, allowing the flavors to meld together.

5. Meanwhile, spread out the sliced potatoes on a separate sheet of heavy-duty aluminum foil. Drizzle with olive oil and sprinkle with salt and pepper. Fold the foil into a packet, ensuring it's sealed well.
6. Place the foil packet of seasoned potatoes on the grill grate over the fire. Cook for about 20-25 minutes, or until the potatoes are tender and slightly crispy.
7. Once the potatoes are cooked, remove the foil packet from the fire and carefully open it.
8. To assemble, layer the cooked chili over the campfire fries and sprinkle with shredded cheddar cheese. Let the heat from the chili and fries melt the cheese.
9. Garnish with sliced green onions and a dollop of sour cream, if desired.

Serve the delicious Campfire Chili Cheese Fries hot, and enjoy!

Note: Feel free to customize this recipe by adding your favorite toppings like jalapeños, chopped tomatoes, or guacamole. You can also adjust the seasoning and spice level to your preference.

Camping Hack #1

DIY Portable Campfire Grill

This DIY portable campfire grill is a cost-effective solution for cooking over an open fire while camping. It's lightweight, easy to assemble, and allows for convenient outdoor cooking. Enjoy your delicious meals while embracing the great outdoors!

Materials needed:

- A sturdy metal cooling rack (with small grid spacing)
- A coat hangers or thick wire
- Pliers or wire cutters

Instructions:

1. Begin by straightening out the coat hangers or thick wire using pliers or wire cutters. You will need two pieces of wire for this hack.
2. Take one wire and bend it into a U-shape, with the ends forming the legs of the grill.
3. Repeat the process with the second wire, creating another U-shape.
4. Position the cooling rack horizontally and place one U-shaped wire on each side of the cooling rack, aligning the legs with the corners.
5. Use pliers or wire cutters to bend the excess wire around the corners of the cooling rack, securing the legs in place. Ensure that the legs are stable and won't easily tip over.
6. Your DIY portable campfire grill is now ready to use!
7. To set it up, find a suitable spot in your campfire area. Make sure the ground is clear of any debris or flammable materials.

8. Place the grill over the campfire, making sure the legs are firmly in the ground and the cooling rack is stable.
9. You can now cook your food directly on the grill, whether it's burgers, veggies, or marshmallows for toasting.

Note: Always follow campfire safety guidelines and regulations when setting up and using a campfire grill. Ensure that the fire is completely extinguished before leaving the area.

Campfire Foil Pack Tacos

Gather around the campfire and savor the deliciousness of these Campfire Foil Pack Tacos. The combination of seasoned meat, veggies, and toppings will make your outdoor lunch extra special. Enjoy the flavors and the company!

Ingredients:

- Ground beef or turkey (or vegetarian substitute)
- Taco seasoning
- Diced bell peppers
- Diced onions
- Corn kernels
- Canned black beans, drained and rinsed
- Shredded cheese (cheddar, Monterey Jack, or a blend)
- Flour tortillas
- Toppings:
- Sliced avocado
- Diced tomatoes
- Chopped cilantro
- Sour cream
- Salsa
- Lime wedges

Instructions:

1. Prepare your campfire and let the flames die down to hot coals.
2. In a skillet, cook the ground beef or turkey (or vegetarian substitute) until browned. Drain any excess fat.
3. Add the diced bell peppers, onions, corn kernels, and black beans to the skillet. Stir in the taco seasoning, following the

package instructions for the right amount of seasoning and water.

4. Simmer the mixture over the fire for a few minutes until the flavors meld together.
5. Tear off large sheets of heavy-duty aluminum foil (one sheet per foil pack).
6. Place a couple of spoonfuls of the taco meat mixture onto the center of each sheet of foil.
7. Sprinkle shredded cheese on top of the meat mixture.
8. Fold the foil over the filling, creating a packet. Seal the edges tightly, leaving a little space for steam to escape.
9. Place the foil packets on the hot coals of the campfire or use a grill grate over the fire.
10. Cook the foil packets for about 10-15 minutes, or until the cheese is melted and the ingredients are heated through.
11. Carefully remove the foil packets from the fire and let them cool for a minute or two.
12. Open the packets and assemble your tacos by spooning the filling onto warm flour tortillas.
13. Top with sliced avocado, diced tomatoes, chopped cilantro, sour cream, salsa, and a squeeze of lime juice.
14. Serve the delicious Campfire Foil Pack Tacos and enjoy the handheld flavor explosion!
15. Note: Feel free to customize your tacos with additional toppings like shredded lettuce, sliced jalapeños, or hot sauce. You can also use hard taco shells if preferred.

Camping Hack #2

DIY Camping Washing Machine

This DIY camping washing machine is a simple and effective way to clean your clothes while camping. It's ideal for smaller loads and can be done with minimal water and resources. Stay fresh and clean on your outdoor adventures!

Materials needed:

- Large, sturdy bucket with a lid
- Plunger (new and dedicated to this purpose)
- Water
- Laundry detergent (camping-friendly or eco-friendly)
- Clothesline or drying rack (optional)

Instructions:

Find a large, sturdy bucket with a tight-fitting lid. This will serve as your camping washing machine.

Fill the bucket halfway with water. Adjust the amount of water based on the size of your laundry load.

Add a small amount of camping-friendly or eco-friendly laundry detergent to the water. Follow the detergent's instructions for the appropriate amount.

Place your clothes into the soapy water in the bucket.

Take the plunger and insert it into the bucket, using it as an agitator.

Move the plunger up and down vigorously for several minutes, agitating the clothes and creating a washing action.

After agitating, let the clothes soak in the soapy water for a few minutes.

Drain the soapy water from the bucket. You can do this by tipping the bucket carefully or using a spigot if your bucket has one.

Refill the bucket with clean water and use the plunger to agitate the clothes again, rinsing out any remaining soap.

Drain the rinse water from the bucket.

Remove the clothes from the bucket and wring them out to remove excess water.

Hang the clothes on a clothesline or drying rack to air dry, or lay them flat on a clean surface.

Note: Make sure to use environmentally friendly soaps and detergents, and dispose of the wash water appropriately, following Leave No Trace principles.

Campfire Apple Crisp Foil Packets

Indulge in the cozy and comforting flavors of this Campfire Apple Crisp. The tender apples, cinnamon-spiced filling, and crispy oat topping create a perfect sweet treat for your campfire evenings. Enjoy the warm and delicious goodness!

Ingredients:

- 2 apples, peeled, cored, and sliced
- 1 tablespoon lemon juice
- 2 tablespoons brown sugar
- 1/4 teaspoon ground cinnamon
- Pinch of nutmeg
- Pinch of salt
- 1/2 cup old-fashioned oats
- 2 tablespoons all-purpose flour
- 2 tablespoons cold butter, cubed
- Optional toppings:
- Vanilla ice cream
- Caramel sauce

Instructions:

1. Prepare your campfire and let the flames die down to hot coals.
2. In a bowl, toss the sliced apples with lemon juice to prevent browning.
3. In another bowl, combine brown sugar, ground cinnamon, nutmeg, and salt. Mix well.
4. Add the apple slices to the sugar-spice mixture and toss until the apples are coated evenly.

5. Tear off two large sheets of heavy-duty aluminum foil (one sheet per foil packet).

6. Divide the apple mixture evenly between the two sheets of foil, placing it in the center.

7. In a separate bowl, mix together oats, flour, and cold butter cubes using your fingers or a fork. Continue mixing until the mixture resembles coarse crumbs.

8. Sprinkle the oat topping evenly over the apple mixture in each foil packet.

9. Fold the foil over the filling, creating a packet. Seal the edges tightly, leaving a little space for steam to escape.

10. Place the foil packets on the hot coals of the campfire or use a grill grate over the fire.

11. Cook the foil packets for about 15-20 minutes, or until the apples are tender and the topping is golden and crisp.

12. Carefully remove the foil packets from the fire and let them cool for a minute or two.

13. Open the packets and serve the warm and comforting Campfire Apple Crisp.

14. If desired, top with a scoop of vanilla ice cream and drizzle with caramel sauce.

Note: You can add a sprinkle of chopped nuts, such as walnuts or pecans, to the oat topping for extra crunch and flavor.

Camping Hack #3

Roll-Up Clothing Organizer

This roll-up clothing organizer hack helps save space and keeps your clothes organized during your camping trip. It eliminates the need to rummage through your entire backpack or storage area to find the right outfit. Enjoy hassle-free mornings and keep your clothes compact and tidy!

Materials needed:

- Large sealable plastic bags (one for each outfit or clothing category)
- Marker or pen
- Rubber bands or small hair elastics

Instructions:

Before your camping trip, gather the outfits or clothing items you plan to wear each day and sort them into categories (e.g., tops, bottoms, undergarments).

Take a large sealable plastic bag and label it with the day or clothing category using a marker or pen.

Place the corresponding outfit or clothing items inside the labeled plastic bag.

Press out any excess air from the bag, helping to reduce bulk and save space.

Seal the plastic bag, ensuring it is airtight and secure.

Roll up the plastic bag tightly, starting from one end and working your way to the other end.

Secure the rolled-up bag with a rubber band or small hair elastic to keep it compact.

Repeat this process for each outfit or clothing category, using separate plastic bags for each.

Pack the rolled-up clothing organizers in your backpack or camping gear storage area, arranging them vertically to optimize space.

When it's time to get dressed, simply unroll the desired bag, and your clothing items will be neatly organized and ready to wear.

A NOTE FROM TONYA

Thank y'all so much for this amazing journey we've been on with all the fun cozy mystery adventures! We've had so much fun and I can't wait to bring you a lot more of them. When I set out to write about them, I pulled from my experiences from camping, having a camper, and fond memories of camping.

Readers ask me if there's a real place like those in my books. Sadly, no. It's a combination of places I've stayed and would own if I could.
      XOXO ~ Tonya

For a full reading order of Tonya Kappes's Novels, visit
Tonyakappes.com

BOOKS BY TONYA
SOUTHERN HOSPITALITY WITH A SMIDGEN OF HOMICIDE

Camper & Criminals Cozy Mystery Series

All is good in the camper-hood until a dead body shows up in the woods.

BEACHES, BUNGALOWS, AND BURGLARIES
DESERTS, DRIVING, & DERELICTS
FORESTS, FISHING, & FORGERY
CHRISTMAS, CRIMINALS, AND CAMPERS
MOTORHOMES, MAPS, & MURDER
CANYONS, CARAVANS, & CADAVERS
HITCHES, HIDEOUTS, & HOMICIDES
ASSAILANTS, ASPHALT & ALIBIS
VALLEYS, VEHICLES & VICTIMS
SUNSETS, SABBATICAL AND SCANDAL
TENTS, TRAILS AND TURMOIL
KICKBACKS, KAYAKS, AND KIDNAPPING
GEAR, GRILLS & GUNS
EGGNOG, EXTORTION, AND EVERGREEN
ROPES, RIDDLES, & ROBBERIES
PADDLERS, PROMISES & POISON
INSECTS, IVY, & INVESTIGATIONS
OUTDOORS, OARS, & OATH
WILDLIFE, WARRANTS, & WEAPONS
BLOSSOMS, BBQ, & BLACKMAIL
LANTERNS, LAKES, & LARCENY
JACKETS, JACK-O-LANTERN, & JUSTICE
SANTA, SUNRISES, & SUSPICIONS
VISTAS, VICES, & VALENTINES
ADVENTURE, ABDUCTION, & ARREST
RANGERS, RVS, & REVENGE

CAMPFIRES, COURAGE & CONVICTS
TRAPPING, TURKEY & THANKSGIVING
GIFTS, GLAMPING & GLOCKS
ZONING, ZEALOTS, & ZIPLINES
HAMMOCKS, HANDGUNS, & HEARSAY
QUESTIONS, QUARRELS, & QUANDARY
WITNESS, WOODS, & WEDDING
ELVES, EVERGREENS, & EVIDENCE
MOONLIGHT, MARSHMALLOWS, & MANSLAUGHTER
BONFIRE, BACKPACKS, & BRAWLS

Killer Coffee Cozy Mystery Series

Welcome to the Bean Hive Coffee Shop where the gossip is just as hot as the coffee.

SCENE OF THE GRIND
MOCHA AND MURDER
FRESHLY GROUND MURDER
COLD BLOODED BREW
DECAFFEINATED SCANDAL
A KILLER LATTE
HOLIDAY ROAST MORTEM
DEAD TO THE LAST DROP
A CHARMING BLEND NOVELLA (CROSSOVER WITH MAGICAL
CURES MYSTERY)
FROTHY FOUL PLAY
SPOONFUL OF MURDER
BARISTA BUMP-OFF
CAPPUCCINO CRIMINAL
MACCHIATO MURDER

Holiday Cozy Mystery Series

CELEBRATE GOOD CRIMES!

FOUR LEAF FELONY
MOTHER'S DAY MURDER
A HALLOWEEN HOMICIDE
NEW YEAR NUISANCE
CHOCOLATE BUNNY BETRAYAL
FOURTH OF JULY FORGERY
SANTA CLAUSE SURPRISE
APRIL FOOL'S ALIBI

Kenni Lowry Mystery Series

Mysteries so delicious it'll make your mouth water and leave you hankerin' for more.

FIXIN' TO DIE
SOUTHERN FRIED
AX TO GRIND
SIX FEET UNDER
DEAD AS A DOORNAIL
TANGLED UP IN TINSEL
DIGGIN' UP DIRT
BLOWIN' UP A MURDER
HEAVENS TO BRIBERY

Magical Cures Mystery Series

Welcome to Whispering Falls where magic and mystery collide.

A CHARMING CRIME
A CHARMING CURE
A CHARMING POTION (novella)
A CHARMING WISH

A CHARMING SPELL
A CHARMING MAGIC
A CHARMING SECRET
A CHARMING CHRISTMAS (novella)
A CHARMING FATALITY
A CHARMING DEATH (novella)
A CHARMING GHOST
A CHARMING HEX
A CHARMING VOODOO
A CHARMING CORPSE
A CHARMING MISFORTUNE
A CHARMING BLEND (CROSSOVER WITH A KILLER COFFEE COZY)
A CHARMING DECEPTION

Mail Carrier Cozy Mystery Series

Welcome to Sugar Creek Gap where more than the mail is being delivered.

STAMPED OUT
ADDRESS FOR MURDER
ALL SHE WROTE
RETURN TO SENDER
FIRST CLASS KILLER
POST MORTEM
DEADLY DELIVERY
RED LETTER SLAY

About Tonya

Tonya has written over 100 novels, all of which have graced numerous bestseller lists, including the USA Today. *Best known for stories charged with emotion and humor and filled with flawed characters, her novels have garnered reader praise and glowing critical reviews. She lives with her husband and a very spoiled rescue cat named Ro. Tonya grew up in the small southern Kentucky town of Nicholasville. Now that her four boys are grown men, Tonya writes full-time in her camper she calls her SHAMPER (she-camper).*

Learn more about her be sure to check out her website tonyakappes.com. Find her on Facebook, Twitter, BookBub, and Instagram

Sign up to receive her newsletter, where you'll get free books, exclusive bonus content, and news of her releases and sales.

If you liked this book, please take a few minutes to leave a review now! Authors (Tonya included) really appreciate this, and it helps draw more readers to books they might like. Thanks!

Made in United States
Troutdale, OR
03/22/2024

18667953R00106